GUS'S HOME

A MORGAN'S RUN ROMANCE

M. LEE PRESCOTT

Gus's Home

By
M. Lee Prescott

Published by Mt. Hope Press
Copyright 2019, M. Lee Prescott
Cover Design by Ashley Lopez
Formatting by E-book Formatting Fairies

http://www.mleeprescott.com/

This book is a work of fiction. Names, characters, places, and events are products of the author's imagination or are used fictitiously. Any resemblance to actual people (alive or deceased), locales, or events is entirely coincidental.

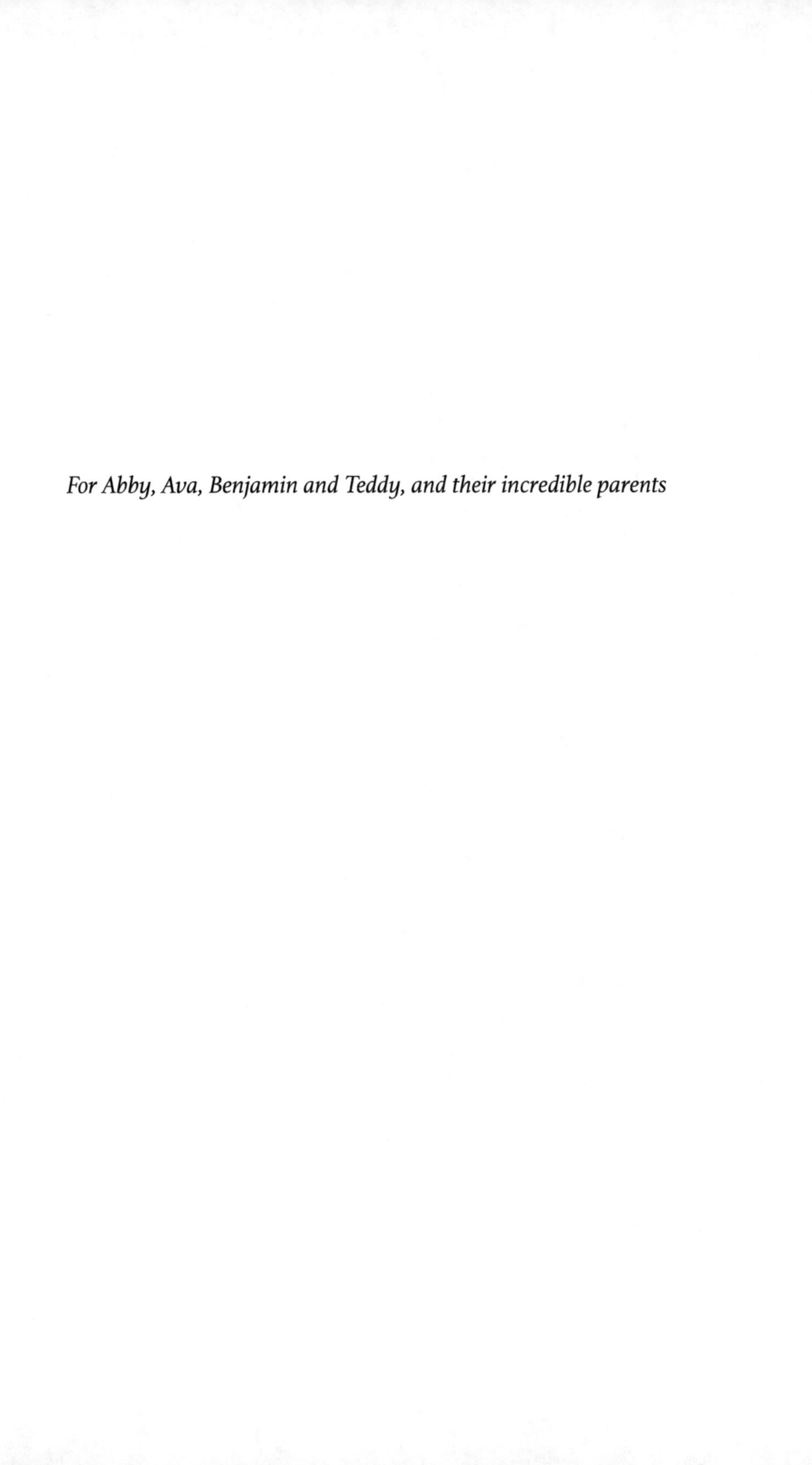

For Abby, Ava, Benjamin and Teddy, and their incredible parents

CHAPTER 1

Gus Casey extracted his wriggling twenty-one-month-old son, Cal, from his car seat as Dulcie, his five-year-old, waited patiently at his side. It had been less than a week since his sister, Laurie, left for Wyoming, and he was going crazy juggling two children and work. *Thank God for the Cottage,* the Morgan's Run day care, where his two went tuition-free. As Cal toddled off toward the Cottage door, Gus took Dulcie's hand. "It'll get better soon, sweetie. I promise."

His daughter nodded but said nothing. Gus worried about her constantly. Cal was plump and strong, but Dulcie never seemed to grow. A tow-haired wisp of a girl, she looked at least a year younger, as if one strong breeze would blow her away. The doctors claimed she was doing well, but still, he worried.

"Morning!" Lynn Manguilli, lead teacher, greeted Cal as the toddler sped by her. She gazed up, smiling at Dulcie, then Gus. "How are the Caseys this morning?"

He gave her a wry smile. "Holdin' on by a thread."

"It'll get easier," she said, smoothing Dulcie's hair as the child hugged her.

"That's what I keep tellin' my sweetheart here," he said. "Now I just have to convince myself."

Lynn watched the handsome horse trainer with arresting green eyes and a grin that could melt an iceberg. His thick sandy hair was tousled as if he'd just rolled out of bed, and she had to repress the urge to comb her fingers through it to settle it down. *Salt of the earth and steady as a rock. A girl could do worse than Gus Casey,* Lynn mused, not for the first time. "You're a great dad. You'll see. You three'll get into a routine of your own now that Laurie's gone. And you can always hire extra help. Willow's around this summer," she said, referring to his boss's eighteen-year-old who was just completing her freshman year of college.

"Yeah, Harley's already suggested that. Thanks. I don't know what we would do without you, Polly, and the Cottage."

Lynn smiled. "You can thank the big bosses for this," she said, referring to Ben Morgan Senior, his wife Leonora, and his college buddy Spark Foster, who had conceived of the idea for the day care center on the Morgans' ranch. They'd also bankrolled it, from construction to the day-to-day running. Teachers' salaries, supplies, and operating expenses were entirely funded by the Morgan-Foster Trust, and tuition was free for the children of all employees of Morgan's Run and Valley Stables, the thoroughbred farm north of town where Gus was assistant trainer.

"Pretty amazing, aren't they?" he said, thinking *so are you.* Lynn was warm and beautiful, and more than once since he'd moved to the Valley, Gus thought about asking her out. *Too good for me, and way too smart* was the conclusion he always reached. Also, too awkward if it didn't work out and the kids still came to the Cottage.

He hung up backpacks, deposited lunches in the kitchen refrigerator, then kissed them both. "Be good," he said to each child. Cal squirmed and ran off to the truck area, and Dulcie nodded, index finger in her mouth. Try as he might, he couldn't break her of the finger-sucking habit. One day at a time, he thought, waving to Polly Granger, Lynn's partner, then stopping at the door to say goodbye to Lynn. "Hope they behave for you."

She patted his arm. "They always do. Don't worry."

Her touch was both comforting and electric. Gus gave her a weary smile and turned away, hoping she hadn't caught the yearning in his gaze.

She had, and it surprised her as it always did. Surprised and unsettled her.

CHAPTER 2

"He's a great guy," Polly said as Lynn shut the door behind Gus. Almost immediately, the door swung open, interrupting them. Kevin Larrabee stepped in as his son, Jasper, flew by, headed for the block corner. "Hi again, guys," she said, smiling at her husband as her stepson disappeared.

Larrabee laughed. "It's been a wild one since you left, Poll."

"Uh-oh."

"It was one of those 'I don't have to wear clothes and you can't make me' mornings. You have his lunch, right?"

Polly smiled. "All set." Still a newlywed, she wanted to jump into his arms and kiss him all better. Instead, she patted his arm, wondering again what he'd say if her suspicions were correct. Her husband was a loving, devoted father, but Jasper was a handful. Now she was two weeks late and feeling a little queasy. Was her sweet, wonderful, long-time bachelor husband ready for a baby *and* an active, often defiant four-year-old?

Kevin kissed her on the cheek and said, "Gotta run, babe. See you tonight." With that, he headed out, closing the door behind him.

"You haven't told him yet?" Lynn asked, watching her colleague.

"There's nothing to tell."

"Have you done the test?"

"No."

"Do you have it?"

"Yes."

"Then just do it, Poll. Better to know one way or the other."

"I'm afraid he's gonna freak. We just got married! This could have happened on the honeymoon for all I know since my cycle is so irregular. I could be four or five months along. That won't even give him or us time to get adjusted."

"If Ben and Maggie Morgan can do it, I'm sure you'll be fine. Ben the third is every bit as rambunctious as Jaspie."

"But he doesn't have a baby brother or sister, and Emma is the most incredibly helpful big sister in the world."

"Speaking of that awesome girl, here she comes," Lynn said, waving as the door opened and Maggie Morgan swept in with her two. "Mornin', Em, Bennie."

"Hi, Lynn, hi, Polly!" Emma said brightly as her brother brushed by to join Jasper, who had already built a four-foot-tall block structure. Like their gorgeous parents, the two Morgan children had luscious brown curls, Emma's now tamed in two long braids. Maggie and her husband, Ben, the eldest of the Morgan siblings, were often referred to as the beautiful couple, and the name was apt. Maggie was dressed for work where she ran the Morgan's Run Stables, her curvaceous figure apparent even in jeans and a faded blue ranch T-shirt.

"Morning, ladies," Maggie said. "I see the gang's all here. Ben Senior'll be by soon for Emma. If not him, Leonora. I've got an early lesson. Okay if I hand you Bennie's things?"

"Of course."

"Emma can put his lunch box in the fridge," Maggie said, leaning down to kiss the top of her daughter's head. "Bye, sweetie. Have fun at school."

Emma threw her arms around her mother. "Bye, Mommy. I love you!"

"Love you too, baby. Say bye to your brother for me, okay? Thanks, Lynn, Poll. Have a great day!"

As the door closed behind her mother, Emma skipped off to the kitchen with the lunch box. She then went to sit with Cal, who was pulling stuffed animals out of baskets on one of the low shelves.

There were seven Cottage regulars, but two-year-old Lily Dillon, daughter of Beth Morgan and Lang Dillon, only came three days, as did one-year-old Charlotte Langdon, Ruthie Morgan and Harley's daughter. Besides Ben, Jasper, Dulcie, and Cal, three-year-old Christy Perez, daughter of one of the ranch workers, came five days. Most days, Emma, Fara, Christy's older sister, and Toby Barnes, son of Maggie's coworker, Jeb, came after school from three to five thirty. Polly and Lynn were the lead teachers, and they had a full-time assistant, Rusty Spalding, a recent University of Arizona early childhood education graduate. At the moment, Rusty sat in the doll corner with Dulcie Casey and Christy. They appeared to be playing Barbie. Capable, down-to-earth, and just plain fun, Rusty had been a welcome addition, as was Willow Goldstein, daughter of Harley Langdon, who would be working with them during her college's summer break.

"So?" Lynn asked, gazing over at Polly as they set out paper plates, popsicle sticks, and glue for the morning's craft project. "I can finish setting up. Why don't you pop in the bathroom now and do the test?"

Polly flushed bright red. "Absolutely not!"

Lynn stared at her. "Okay, partner, what's wrong?"

Tears filling her green eyes, Polly turned away and headed to the kitchen. Lynn gazed over her shoulder. "Rusty? You got this for five?" He gave her a thumbs-up as she stepped into the kitchen and partially closed the door. Her colleague and former roommate was now slumped in a chair, elbows on the table, head in hands. "Hey, Poll, what is it? You okay?"

"No... Yes... I don't know." She shook her head, sitting up, wiping her eyes. "This is me these days. One minute gloriously happy, the next minute a basket case."

"They say that happens with hormones and all," Lynn said, patting her back as she came round to sit beside her. "Are you worried about Kevin?"

"No, he'll be thrilled. Overwhelmed, but thrilled."

"Then?"

"Can you imagine what my parents will say, especially my mom? And, even if she didn't say anything, I'm not sure I can do it, with my heart and all. The doctors weren't encouraging." Polly had been born with ventricular septal defect (VSD), which involved a small hole in her heart. Several surgeries over the years had corrected the condition and closed the hole, but a vulnerability still existed, particularly, she had been told, when women get pregnant.

Lynn took her friend's hand. "All the more reason to find out now, talk to Kev, and then see the doctor. The sooner the better, sweetie."

"I know, I know... I guess I just wanted to hold on to the dream for a little while before they take him or her away."

"You don't know that," Lynn said, aware of a ruckus coming from the front room. "You stay here and pull yourself together, and I'll see what's happening out there. Take all the time you need."

Lynn emerged to find Jasper and Bennie wrestling on the living room carpet, Ben's grandfather kneeling beside them, endeavoring to break it up. Lynn came to his side and grabbed Jasper while Ben Senior took hold of his red-faced grandson. Emma stood at the side, Cal in her arms. "Ben, stop it! Gramma won't like that at all! I'm gonna tell Daddy if you don't stop right now!"

Ben Senior grinned, still clutching the now sulking four-year-old. "My savior," he said, winking at Lynn. "No worries, baby girl. This ole cowboy can still wrestle a runaway calf." He gazed down at his grandson. "Now listen here, partner. If I let you go, are you gonna behave yourself?"

No response, lip stuck out, scowl on his round cherubic face.

"Okay, then. I guess yer sister and I'll have to stay all day to watch out for you. Can't have you and your little cowpoke friend botherin' all the other kids."

Jasper sat on Lynn's lap, a similar scowl on his face. This standoff lasted for several minutes until Bennie looked up at his grandfather. "I sorry."

Ben Senior grinned, winking at Emma. "How 'bout yer buddy?"

Jasper gazed at the floor. "Sorry."

"What d'ya think, Lynn? Safe to let these hombres out of jail now?" Ben asked.

Lynn smiled at him, then turned her attention on the boys. "Ben, Jasper, you know the rule about wrestling, right?"

Small nods.

"Well, this is your last chance today. If it happens again, you guys will have to have a time out, then not play together for a while. Is that clear?"

More nodding.

"Okay, then," she said, releasing Jasper as Ben Senior let Bennie down.

"Come on, Em. You'll be late for school if we don't hurry," the Morgan patriarch said, grinning at Lynn. "If you have any more trouble, give me a call. Spark and I can come back and corral the little varmints for you."

Lynn laughed. "Much as I'd like to hire you guys full-time, I'm sure we can handle things from here. Thanks. Have a great day. You too, Em! We're doing Hula-Hooping this afternoon when you guys get off the bus. See ya!"

CHAPTER 3

Both Lynn and Polly stayed late. Maggie took Jasper to their house for a playdate, and the last pickup was Gus Casey. "Hey," he said, stepping in, his jacket covered with grass stains and dust. "How was the day?"

He looks exhausted, Lynn thought, *and now he goes home to full-time parenting, poor guy. Exhausted, but still pretty darn cute.* "They were great, as always."

"Naps?"

"Both of them. Cal slept for three hours, Dulcie about an hour. This is a sleeping crew, though. After morning, lunch, and recess, they're *all* ready to conk out. Teachers too," she said, smiling. "You look like you've had a long day."

"New horses, foaling, you name it, we were doin' it. May have to be fast food for this crew tonight."

Before she knew what she was saying, Lynn blurted out, "I have burgers and hot dogs at my house. You're welcome to come there for a quick dinner."

Stunned for an instant, he recovered and gave her a grateful smile. "Thanks, but not sure that's the best idea on a work day. Besides, I'm covered with crap, and I need a shower."

"We live five minutes apart. Here's my address and cell number," she said, grabbing a crayon and scribbling on a scrap of paper. "Why don't we say this. If you get home, get showered, and want to pop over for a quick bite, give a call and I can have dinner waiting on the table when you arrive. If I don't hear from you, everything'll be there for another day."

"You sure?" he asked, green eyes studying her.

"Yup. Now take these guys home while I help Polly clean up."

As the door closed behind Gus and his children, Polly peeked out from the kitchen. "That was smooth."

"I don't know what came over me!" Lynn said, face reddening.

"I do. He's a nice handsome guy and you're a beautiful single woman. Why shouldn't you have dinner?"

"With the kids?"

Polly laughed. "It's a start!"

"Hmm... Well, I'd better get cracking," Lynn said.

"Can you wait five minutes?" Polly asked, the moment's gaiety drained from her face.

"Of course," Lynn said as her partner headed for the bathroom with a long, thin box.

A few minutes later, Polly emerged. Lynn looked up, and she nodded.

"Positive?"

"Yup."

Lynn crossed the room and wrapped her in a bear hug. "Congratulations! Now go home, tell your husband, celebrate, and decide next steps."

"Thanks, Lynn. Have a fun dinner."

The phone rang five minutes after Lynn stepped into her condo. "Hey, it's Gus. Is the invitation still open for tonight?"

"Absolutely!" she said.

"Give us half an hour to shower and take baths, and we'll be there. Okay if the kids are in pj's?"

"Of course," she said, smiling as she rang off. *Now to make myself beautiful and make dinner in thirty minutes or less!*

Hamburgers and hot dogs were on the grill when the doorbell rang. Lynn had showered and changed into skinny jeans and a flowing tunic, the dark colors accentuating her sparkling charcoal eyes. Her thick, dark hair fell loosely around her shoulders and down her back, and silver hoop earrings and an assortment of silver bracelets jangled as she grabbed hold of the doorknob. She felt sexy as she swung open the door, finding the little family on her doorstep. "Welcome, come in!"

Lynn stepped aside as Gus carried Cal in, Dulcie by his side. She caught the heady scent of his aftershave, citrusy and musky, as he set Cal down and handed her a bottle of Pinot Noir. "It's from Saguaro Vineyards," he said. "S'posed to be pretty good."

Lynn smiled. "It is, thanks."

"Anything precious and breakable within Cal's reach?"

She smiled. "I run a day care center, remember? So, the burgers and dogs are almost ready. Would the kids like something to drink? Water? Juice? Lemonade? I have milk too."

"Water'd be great," he said. "I've got their sippy cups. This is a great place you have here. Look, kids, the river." He pointed to the glass slider. "May we?"

"Of course, go out. We have a nice backyard. They can explore while I finish grilling."

Gus took the two children, and they ran around the small grassy area, Dulcie holding her brother's hand. "Can I help?" he asked, turning to Lynn.

"Only if you'd like to get *us* something to drink. I have beer in the fridge, or there's the wine."

He grinned. "Confession? I'm not much of a wine drinker, but I would take a beer."

"Please, go in and grab one for yourself and me. I'll keep an eye on the kids." She watched him step around her and head in. His broad shoulders strained the fabric of a freshly pressed pale-blue dress shirt. His khakis were also pressed and appeared brand-new.

Only his running shoes showed signs of serious wear and tear. Gus Casey was a solid, handsome man not much taller than herself. His thick sandy hair was in need of a trim, but she loved longer hair on men. As he handed her a bottle of Desert Amber, a local brew, his fingers brushed against hers, sending shivers up her spine. *Whoa girl,* she mused, mumbling "thanks" before turning back to the grill.

"You look pretty," he said.

Startled, she blushed. "Thank you. You look pretty good yourself."

"Only so much you can do with this," he said, throwing open his hands. "Thanks for having us. We don't get out much."

"Takes a while to settle into the Valley, but people are pretty friendly."

"Yup."

"Do you like working at Valley Stables?" she asked, referring to the new thoroughbred breeding and training facility north of town. A lifelong dream of Ben Morgan Senior and his college buddy Spark Foster, it was run by Harley Langdon, former boss of Morgan's Run Stables and husband of Ruthie Morgan, the youngest of Ben and Leonora Morgan's children.

"It's a great place. Terrific bosses, great coworkers. It's gonna be something when everything's up and running. We've got some really promising horses."

"Yeah, Ben and Spark are remarkable, aren't they?"

"Harley and Tom too," he said, referring to Langdon and his immediate boss, head trainer Tom Jacobi, the latter whom Lynn had had a serious crush on. Her interest, however, had not been reciprocated. She'd finally given up and admitted to herself that the ruggedly handsome foreman could not be *less* interested in her.

"It takes a while, but you'll be part of the community in no time. The Morgans and Fosters make sure everyone is included in everything. Once you're here, you're family."

You're right about that, he thought watching her. His wife, Lisbeth, had been a little slip of a thing. He always said, like her daughter, that a breeze would knock her flat. Cal's birth had done just that. She had died within minutes of her son's first cries. This woman was Lisbeth's polar opposite. Big-boned and curvaceous, she was dark and sexy, in contrast to Lisbeth's thin frailty. *Here is a woman who could carry the burden of the world on her shoulders. We could sure use her strength.*

"Have you experienced a Valley wedding yet? Or, should I say, one put on by either the Morgans or Spark?"

"No. We were newly arrived when Polly and Kevin got married. They invited us, but Dulcie was sick and I didn't want to leave her."

"Well, hold on to your hat. I'm assuming you're all going to Hope and Robbie's wedding?" She referred to the nuptials of the third Morgan son to Hope Seymour, a prominent Southwest painter.

"I am. We are. I can't believe they included the kids."

Lynn laughed. "Always. That's half the fun. Just wait." It was comfortable talking to Gus. *No pressure, no flirting. Just warm companionship. This might be okay for now. See where it goes, but there was that electricity in his touch.*

After a raucous meal spent endeavoring to keep Cal in his seat and coaxing Dulcie to eat at least a few bites of hot dog, he gazed across at her. "I think we may be nearing the witching hour."

He was rewarded with a genuine warm smile that sent his long-lost libido into overdrive.

"I think you might be right," she said, bringing a wet washcloth to wipe Cal's catsup-smeared face.

She walked them to his truck and helped Dulcie with her car seat. The shy child gave her a smile and hug as she did every morning and afternoon. "Night, sweetie," Lynn said, returning her embrace. "Sleep tight."

Gus came around to her side of the truck. "Thanks for having us. This was really fun." As he spoke, he reached out and hugged her briefly.

Lynn returned the hug, then stepped back, smiling demurely. "It was fun for me too."

"I'm gonna go out on a limb here," he said, meeting her dark eyes. "I have two questions for you. I don't s'pose you'd like to go out to dinner sometime without the kids?"

Surprised but also delighted, she nodded. "I'd love to."

He grinned. "Terrific. I'll call you," he said, turning away.

"Gus?"

"Yup?" he said, turning back to her, still smiling.

"What was your second question?"

"Oh, yeah. Do you know any good babysitters?"

She laughed. "We have a list. I'll give it to you in the morning. I'd recommend trying Willow, Harley's daughter, first. She's due home any day now."

"Thanks."

"Night," she said, waving as he hopped in the truck and started the engine.

People come along when you least expect them, she mused, heading inside, a huge shit-eating grin on her face. She considered calling Polly but decided, with the pregnancy news, that she had enough on her plate.

CHAPTER 4

"That's wonderful!" Polly said. It was early morning, and they were setting up before the children arrived. Lynn had related the highlights of dinner with Gus early the next morning. "He's a really great guy. So happy for you."

"Whoa, girl. It's dinner, not a marriage proposal. I barely know the man. Gus is great, yes, but I'm not sure he's my type, and I'm not sure he's really ready for a relationship. His wife hasn't been gone long, and they were high school, maybe even grade school, sweethearts."

Polly twirled a broom as she stowed it in the corner. "Excuses, excuses!"

She looks happy, thank God, Lynn thought, wondering if she should even ask about last night with Kevin. Finally, she said, "So, you seem lighter today. Did it go okay with Kevin and your news?"

"Yes, it was a relief to tell him. I'll call Dr. Blake this morning. We're going to see him together."

"And my buddy Jasper will be with me."

"Thanks."

"We ready for this morning?" Lynn asked. They were going on a field trip to the ranch's farm, the largest and most successful organic farm in the Southwest, run by two of the Morgan sisters, Beth and

Ruthie. Beth oversaw the entire operation and the marketing, Ruthie ran the farm and herb business, and Raoul Rodriquez managed the farm's livestock. They would be traveling in the tiny school bus equipped with car seats that Spark Foster purchased a month earlier. This was only their second outing, but they hoped to use it almost daily over the summer to transport the children to and from the pool at Emma's Dream, the ranch's summer camp for handicapped children situated a quarter mile down the road from the Cottage.

"Ready as we'll ever be. Lorna Perez is coming with us, so that'll help with Christy. Willow can take charge of Charlotte, and we'll assign Cal to Rusty. I'll take Lily and Dulcie, and you can take the hellions," she said, referring to Ben Morgan the third and Jasper. "They mind you best. Always better that I not take Jasper, as he takes advantage of 'Mommy.' Did I tell you he's started to call me that?"

Lynn smiled. "About a thousand times."

"I know. It feels good, that's all."

"Course it does. He's damn lucky to have you as his mommy." Jasper's biological mother, Judith, died suddenly of a drug overdose a year earlier, not long after she revealed his existence to Kevin. It had been a bumpy road, but Jasper was settling in happily to Valley life. His friendship with little Ben Morgan had been a huge help in the transition. The boys were inseparable.

"Hey, ladies, good morning!" a voice called as Lang Dillon stepped in, Lily, his two-year-old in his arms. "We the first arrivals?"

"You are," Lynn said. "Hi, Lily. We missed you yesterday."

The toddler buried her head in her father's shoulder. Lang flashed his two-hundred-watt smile. "We had a busy day with Granny Dillon yesterday, and we're getting off to a slow start this morning." Ash-blond like his daughter, he had the kind of sky-blue eyes that made women swoon. Tall and lanky with a runner's build, Lang was the owner of a very successful outdoor clothing and gear company, Rambler Sports.

"Hey, Lily, wanta help me with the dollhouse?" Polly called from the playroom.

Lily peeked but then rested her head on her dad's shoulder again, thumb in mouth.

"Guess where we're goin' this morning?" Lynn asked. "To Mommy's farm."

Lily nodded, slowly loosening her grasp on Lang's collar. As she slipped down and headed for the dolls, he said, "Beth's a little worried about it, actually. She's got a busy afternoon and can't take Lily if she freaks out. She can call me, or Leonora said she'd pick her up if she's being clingy."

"No worries."

"She's definitely going through a separation-from-Mommy stage."

"Very normal," Lynn said. "She's always fine here once she gets in the swing."

"Well, I'll hightail it, then. Have a great trip." He stepped in, kissed the top of his daughter's head, and headed out. Lily was already engrossed in play with Polly and her baby doll.

The last arrivals were Gus, Cal, and Dulcie. He looked particularly harried, his hair askew, unshaven, his shirt rumpled. Lynn smiled. Even in his current state, he was gorgeous. *Poor guy.* She found herself wanting to take him in her arms and tell him everything would be all right "someday."

"Sorry. Rough night," he said as he set Cal down. "He ate almost nothing for breakfast. Can he have a snack now?"

"Of course. Want one of ours? Graham crackers? Fruit?"

"Anything's fine, thanks," he said, hanging up their backpacks and handing the lunch boxes to Dulcie. "Put these in the fridge, sweetie. That's Daddy's helper." He started to set their water bottles on the shelf and noticed the rest of the kids' bottles were missing.

"Oh, here, in this bag," Lynn said. "We're going on our farm trip in about half an hour."

"Oh, right, that's today." Gus stopped, shook himself, and grinned. "Sorry, I've been acting like a maniac, haven't I?"

"Just a little," she said, smiling. "But you're entitled."

Just seeing him smile and she went weak at the knees.

"Good morning," he said. "How are you?"

"Fine. Sorry for the rough night."

He shrugged. "It happens. Cal's not a good sleeper, but last night, it was Dulcie. She's been having nightmares. They both ended up in my bed. They'll both nap today."

"Is there a nap room at Valley Stables?"

He laughed. "Don't I wish. Hey, I've actually got some time now 'cause I have to pick up something in town at ten. Do you need help packing everyone into your shiny new bus?"

"That would actually be great. So you'll stay till we leave?"

"Sure." *Anything to be around you,* he thought, watching her unwrap graham crackers and hand one to his son. "This is such an amazing space you've made here for the kids. The Cottage was one of the real selling points for me in moving to Saguaro Valley."

"Anything's possible when you have the deep pockets we have around here."

"Still, this part is yours and Polly's work, the setup and everything. My kids are so happy to come every day."

"It's a pretty great place. As long as the ranch and stables people keep having babies, we'll probably stay in business."

"Are you worried about that? Job security, I mean?"

"No, not at all. I don't know how long I'll be here, but the bosses have a long-term plan. The Cottage will either remain in operation in perpetuity as a town day care or become part of Emma's Dream, maybe a place for counselors or others to stay."

His face fell. "So you're not planning on staying?"

"I didn't say that. It's just, you never know. I love what I'm doing now, but who can say? I love a lot of things. Actually, if Robbie Morgan ever gets an outdoor adventures business up and running, I'd go to work for him in a heartbeat. I'm not much of a horseback rider, but I love to hike."

"Me too," he said, eyes registering surprise. "My wife, Lisbeth, wasn't into hiking, but my brothers and friends did a lot of camping and hiking in high school and college."

"We should go out someday. There are great trails around here, as I'm sure you're aware."

"I'd like that, once I get some regular sitters."

Lynn smiled. "There are plenty of easy, kid-friendly trails. I'm sure those broad, strong shoulders could handle a child pack for Cal."

"I actually have one, but he's not too crazy about it. Doesn't like to be cooped up."

"Let's give it a try. You never know," she said, patting his forearm in a gesture she then decided might have been too intimate. "Hey, Poll, what d'ya think? Start loading the bus? Gus said he'd help."

Polly gazed past her colleague to where Gus Casey sat, feeding Cal a slice of apple, and nodded. "Ready when you are. Shall we change diapers, then head out?"

A few minutes later, they began loading supplies and kids into the bus. The children were beside themselves with excitement at riding in the "real school bus." Gus strapped Cal in, gave him a kiss, then came around to help Dulcie. Still tiny enough that she needed a full car seat, she sat quietly as her father tightened the straps. "Looks good, princess," he said softly as doe eyes gazed up at him. "Hey, sweetie, it's gonna be fun." He followed her eyes, which came to rest on Lorna Perez, seated next to her daughter, Christy. He knew exactly what she was thinking and whom she was missing and *there isn't a damn thing I can do to make it better.* "Hey, princess, I love you. Have fun." He kissed her nose, then her cheek before withdrawing.

After strapping the hellions in, Lynn observed Gus, marveling at his tenderness with his children and others.

"You okay?" Polly asked, coming to stand beside her. "I think we're set. You looked worried. Is something wrong?"

Lynn shook herself. "Nope, right as rain."

"You're driving, right?" Polly asked.

"Yup. All set." She grabbed her backpack from the grass and hopped into the bus.

As she strapped in, Gus came to the driver's side of the bus and tapped the window. Lynn jumped and said, "Oh!" then opened the side window. "Thanks for the help," she stammered.

He regarded her quizzically, then said, "No problem. I'll follow you, help get 'em out, then take off. Okay?"

"Sure, fine, okay, that'd be great. See you up there." Lynn knew she was babbling but couldn't stop herself. *Get a grip, woman!* She started the engine and backed out of the Cottage drive. *He might not be my type, but something's happening, and I'm clearly out of my depth!*

In truth, Lynn had had few boyfriends, and when she did date, she had been the instigator, usually pursuing men who weren't interested in her. This whatever it was with Gus was virgin territory for her. *Friend? Parent-teacher? Dating?* None of the descriptors quite fit, and she found herself unsettled and distracted. *Good thing he's leaving when we get to the farm,* she thought, steering the bus up the winding ranch drive.

Beth and Ruthie were waiting when they drove up beside the farm office. They each took their daughters, then welcomed everyone. As the other adults corralled the group around their hosts, Gus came to Lynn's side. He touched her shoulder lightly, and Lynn felt faint. "I'm heading out. Have fun."

Shaking herself, she turned to him, smiling. "Thanks for all your help." Trying to affect a light tone that she didn't feel at the moment, she added, "You're hired anytime you need a job."

"How about Saturday?"

"Excuse me?"

Amused at her flustered state, he said, "For a hike? It's supposed to be nice."

"That would be... I mean, great, fine. Talk later?"

"Yup." Gus smiled as Lynn turned her attention to Ruthie, who was telling the children about the strawberry patch where they were going first.

Gus couldn't stop grinning as he headed for his truck. *Lynn Manguilli might be too smart, accomplished, and beautiful for an old Wyoming prairie dog like me, but it's sure worth a try!*

CHAPTER 5

Gus met Tom Jacobi at the smaller of the two racetracks. He was watching a rider and horse circle the half-mile oval at a canter. "Morning, boss. How's it going?"

"Great. She looks good, doesn't she?"

"She should."

"Did you pick up the shipment from the Depot?"

"Yup. Who's the rider?"

"Alice Hanley. She's an up-and-comer. Spark wooed her down here for a couple of weeks."

"Sits pretty well, and by the look of it, she's pretty too."

Tom gave his assistant a quizzical look. "You're chipper this morning. What's gotten into you?"

Gus grinned. "Life."

"Well, you'd better take that life into the barn and bring out Stella. Harley wants Alice to give her a good workout."

"Is that wise? Stella's only been here two days."

Tom shrugged. "Time will tell. He's the big boss."

Gus considered arguing, but then headed for the barn. He met Harley in the side yard, Stella at his side. He was tightening her saddle. "Hey, Gus. Ready to give this gal a run around?"

"I'm not sure she's ready."

Harley petted the thoroughbred's flank, receiving a soft nicker, then a nudge from the tall chestnut mare. "She's a direct descendant of the Godolphin Arabian. I think she can handle a little trot around the track, don't you?"

Gus shrugged. "You're the boss."

Harley studied the young trainer. He trusted him and his instincts. Since he couldn't steal Nick Parker, the resident horse whisperer from Morgan's Run Stables, he had been thrilled the first time he'd seen Gus with a horse. "Yeah, but I want your two cents, always. You worried?"

Gus patted Stella's nose, and she leaned into him, man and horse already bonded. "Tell the hotshot jockey to take it easy, and she should be fine."

"Okay, then."

"Hey, Harley. I saw Willow at the Cottage this morning."

"Yup, she's home for the summer, living with us."

"Think she'd still be interested in sitting?"

"Probably, sure. You got a hot date?"

Gus grinned. "Maybe."

"Give her a call. Her roommate is staying with us too. She's working at the camp, but she'd probably be interested. Peggy's an education major, I think. Willow can give you her cell, or just call the house. I think she's pretty much lazing around the next two weeks before camp opens."

"Thanks, Harley."

His boss grinned, giving him a look. "You didn't say who your date was. Anyone I know?"

"She's a friend, really."

"Uh-huh. That's always the way it starts."

"Lynn from the day care."

"She's good people."

"Yes."

"Charlotte's crazy about her and Polly."

"My two as well."

"Well, good luck with that. Can you take Stella out? I've gotta check in with Patty. Since our resident vet flew the coop, things have been a little crazy."

Gus nodded, taking the horse's reins. In his opinion, Dr. Patty Turner, the assistant vet under Kyle Morgan, was not ready for the job that had been thrust upon her since the youngest Morgan son had moved east with his fiancée. She had neither the temperament nor the patience for large animal care, and he wondered for the hundredth time why she'd ever applied for the position. *She'd be better with cats, dogs, and hamsters,* he mused, leading Stella toward the track. *Thank God for Ned Williams.* Maggie Morgan's dad stopped in almost every day. Years earlier, Ned had almost completed veterinary school when life pulled him away, and he never got a degree. The Valley's most famous wrangler, he was also its most steady and reliable large animal physician.

"Here she is," he said, opening the gate as Alice Hanley dismounted. Leo, the charcoal-gray stallion, whinnied, pulling back, rearing slightly. "Whoa, boy," Gus said, stepping between the jockey and horse. Instantly, Leo settled and stood docilely at his side.

"Hey, pretty girl," the petite jockey said, rubbing Stella's nose. "You're more my style."

In one fluid motion, she mounted, took hold of the reins, and flicked her waist-length blonde braid over her shoulder.

Gus watched the jockey. *She is pretty and she knows it.* "Hey, Ms. Hanley. Go easy, okay?"

"Are you honestly telling me how to ride?"

"No, I'm honestly telling you how to treat this horse. She's just arrived, and she's still settling in."

"Tom?" Alice asked, turning to his boss.

"Gus is the expert here. Easy does it, okay? Just exercise."

The jockey rolled her brown eyes, then nudged Stella onto the track. The beautiful mare followed her lead, and they were soon cantering around the half-mile track. As they watched, Tom shook his head. "If Stella's half what they say she is, Ben and Spark have a winner here."

"Yup," Gus said, watching rider and horse. *If they treat her right.*

CHAPTER 6

Alice Hanley and Stella were just finishing the workout when Ben Morgan Senior drove in. He and a stranger, who looked vaguely familiar, hopped out of his Rover. They approached the group leaning on the fence. "Mornin', men. How's it goin'?"

"Great," Tom replied, tipping his hat.

"I'd like you all to meet my baby brother, Richard. Visiting from back east for the wedding."

They all came forward to shake hands. Like his older brother, Richard Morgan was tall and slender with salt and pepper hair, bushy eyebrows and a broad grin. His eyes were coal black, and they twinkled when he smiled, perhaps more mischievously than his brother's.

Richard Morgan gazed around. "What a place these tycoons built, huh? And who's this fine filly?" he asked as Alice and Stella approached.

"Stella. She's one of our newest additions," his brother said, as proud as a new father. "We have high hopes for her."

"I can see why," Richard said, eyes moving from rider to horse.

Ben chuckled. "Alice Hanley, my brother Richard."

"Dick, please," he said, moving to greet Alice. "Need a pair of hands?"

"Thanks, but I'm fine," she said as she slid effortlessly to the ground. After handing Stella's reins to Gus, she shook Richard's hand, then excused herself.

As the men watched her departure, Tom said, "Don't take offense. She's great with the horses and an exceptional rider, just not very social."

"Who cares if she's a card-carrying hermit as long as she's a winner?" Richard said, patting his brother's back. "Now, let's have that grand tour."

As the older men departed, Gus turned to Tom. "That's a surprise. Not that I know what's what, but didn't know Mr. Morgan had a brother."

Tom shrugged. "According to Harley, they lost touch and have just reconnected."

AFTER THEY LOADED THE CHILDREN BACK IN THE COTTAGE BUS, RUTHIE and Beth stood chatting with Lynn while the group waited for Rusty and Polly to take Bennie and Jasper to the bathroom. Leonora had met them and taken Charlotte and Lily back to the Big House for the day. "I think she wants to show them off to Uncle Dick," Beth said.

Ruthie rolled her eyes. "Don't know why. He doesn't really seem like the kid type. He'll probably scare Charlotte with those bushy eyebrows."

"Ruthie!" her sister said, jabbing her. "Be nice. Besides, after eight of his own, I imagine he loves kids."

"Is he visiting for the wedding?" Lynn asked.

Ruthie shrugged. "Apparently. None of us, except Beth and Ben, even remember him."

"He's lived overseas most of his life," Beth said.

Another eye roll from the youngest Morgan sibling. "Not the past twenty years."

"He's a bit eccentric," Beth said, smiling. "He's brought two of our cousins with him, which is wonderful. You'll meet 'em soon enough. You're coming to Spark's prewedding clambake, aren't you?"

Lynn laughed. "Yes, but I still can't believe it's happening. Clambake out here?"

Beth smiled. "You know Spark. Loves any excuse for a party and always likes to top his last shindig. I believe our dad is egging him on and probably helping fund it since it's out at the new farm."

"Harley's having fits," Ruthie said, a mischievous gleam in her blue eyes. "Thinks the tent and all the commotion will unsettle the new horses. Oh boy, here come the monsters," she added as Jasper and her nephew banged out the office door and chased each other to the bus. Rusty and Polly followed in their wake.

"Thanks again," Lynn said to the sisters. "This was really fun."

"Our pleasure," Beth said.

"They can come every day as far as I'm concerned," Ruthie said, reaching in to ruffle Dulcie's hair. "We've got some champion strawberry pickers in this crew. Especially one young lady I know." Dulcie rewarded her with a huge smile. "Now remember, guys and gals, we'll have a monster game of tag out at the horse farm this Saturday, right?" A chorus of yeahs rang out.

Lynn chuckled. "It's official. Spark's clambake'll be a blowout."

"Where are they getting the clams?" Rusty asked as they drove down the hill to the Cottage.

"Kevin told me that everything is being shipped from Maine," Polly said. "I think Mr. Morgan's brother, Richard, has helped with this. Apparently, shipping seafood all over the world is one of his many businesses."

"Never a dull moment around here," Lynn said. "I, for one, can't wait for a big bowl of steamers."

"And lobsters," Polly added.

"I've never had either," Willow said.

"Well then, get ready for a treat!" Lynn said as she pulled the bus out onto the Cottage drive.

CHAPTER 7

Saturday dawned clear and warm. A perfect morning for a hike. As Gus pulled up in the truck a little after nine, Lynn was waiting, a small pack at her side. "Morning!" she called, slipping into the cab, turning to greet each child, then smiling at their father. "You guys ready?"

Dulcie gave her a shy smile, and Cal clapped his hands.

"More importantly, are you ready?" Gus asked, smiling at her. "I mean, you do this all week. Sure you don't want a peaceful morning?"

"I'm really excited," she said, reaching back to pat Dulcie's knee.

Gus gave her a grateful look, then pulled the truck out of the lot. "Here we go, then!"

As they drove the short distance to the trailhead, Lynn was acutely aware of his nearness in a way that unsettled and excited her. *Why do I feel this way? He's the steadiest guy I know.* To break the silence and settle her racing thoughts, she asked, "So is the circus tent up and ready for tonight's shindig?"

"Tents, you mean? There's the main tent with all the tables, then several serving tents, as well as two huge bake pits. Apparently, they started the fire to heat the rocks at five this morning."

"Can't wait."

"I've never had clams or lobster."

"Really?"

"They're not a popular menu item in Wyoming."

She smiled. "I suppose not. I grew up with them. My dad's favorite meal. We had at least two beach clambakes every summer."

"Not sure about how the kids'll react."

"Not to worry. If I know Spark, there'll be hamburgers and hot dogs and a bunch of other things for the kids. I doubt very much his grandson, Toby, or most of the other kids will touch a clam. Turn right here," she said, indicating a small dirt parking area to the right.

Gus parked, then hauled out the large child carrier pack as Lynn helped the kids out of their car seats.

As Cal circled the truck, laughing and waving his arms, Gus said, "What d'ya think? Should I let him walk a while and see how it goes?"

"Why not? It's pretty flat. You can put your water bottles and snacks in my pack. I've got plenty of room." She turned her back to him. "Just unzip the top and stuff 'em in."

Gus grabbed the kids' sippy bottles and his metal one and unzipped her pack. After zipping it back up, he squeezed her shoulder. "Thanks."

His touch sent shivers down her spine, and she blushed. "Okay then, we're ready, kids!" she said cheerfully as she led the way toward the woods.

For twenty minutes or so, Cal skipped beside his sister. Dulcie seemed to draw energy from the thick woods, her cheeks rosy, eyes bright.

"This is a real treat for us," he said. "Thanks for suggesting it."

"You've got to stop thanking me every five minutes. It's a treat for me too. Since Polly moved out, I've been kind of a recluse on the weekends."

"I would think you'd have plenty of friends."

"Back home, not here. Don't get me wrong. Everyone's great and I get invited to all the big dinners and parties at the Morgans' and Spark's. It's just most Valley people, at least the ones I know, are married or with partners. I still do things with Polly, but she's super involved with Kevin and Jasper now. Sometimes I'll meet Aria, Spark's cook, for a drink, or I've done things with a couple of the women who work at the ranch spa. Other than that, my social life is pretty dull."

"Social life? What's that?" he said, smiling.

"Do you regret leaving Wyoming?"

"No, there wasn't much there for me. My family, yes, but they have their own lives. I have a couple of buddies, but Lissie and I had been together so long that we were each other's social life."

"Must've been very hard."

"It was and still is."

"What was she like?"

"Lissie?"

Lynn nodded, not sure she wanted to hear the answer.

"She was quiet, like Dulcie, and kind. Not a mean bone in her body. She was a teacher, but gave it up to stay home when she got pregnant with Cal. She was real sick from the beginning, but never complained."

"Was it morning sickness?"

He gazed ahead, checking on the kids, who were picking yellow flowers from the side of the trail. "She was about six months, and she couldn't get out of bed one morning. I insisted we see the doctor, and they ran a bunch of tests. She had placenta previa, and they recommended bed rest. She tried, but Dulcie was a toddler. My family, especially Laurie, my sister, helped out as much as they could. The doctors wanted to hospitalize her and take the baby, but she wouldn't hear of it.

"Cal was born a few weeks early. He came suddenly, and she hemorrhaged. They delivered the baby but couldn't stop the bleeding. Lissie died not long after Cal was born." Gus's eyes had filled, and he looked away.

"I'm so sorry. I didn't mean to pry. What a terrible loss for you."

"When Lissie died, the light went out in Dulcie's eyes. Maybe mine too."

"Daddy, look!" his daughter called, her arms full of yellow oleander.

"Those are poisonous, aren't they?" he said.

"Only if they eat them. Just to be safe, we'll wash their hands before they have a snack."

"They're beautiful, princess! What's your brother got there?"

"Sticks and mud," she said, making a face.

"Let's catch up to him, then," Gus said, patting her head, then taking the proffered bouquet and handing it to Lynn.

"This is so great for her. I should get out here more often."

"It's pretty," Lynn said. "If you want easy trails, you can pretty much follow the river either north or south. Those paths go on for days."

"Next time?" He looked over at her.

Lynn met his eyes. "Next time."

As the trail began to climb, Cal started whining.

"In about a half mile, there's a really nice clearing where we can stop to eat," Lynn said as Gus lifted Cal in his arms.

"What d'ya think, buddy? Wanta ride with Dad for a while?"

Lynn helped to settle the toddler in the pack and hoisted it onto Gus's back. As she adjusted the straps, he turned, and his cheek brushed hers. "Sorry," she said.

"I'm not," he said, his eyes warm.

She blushed and stepped ahead, taking Dulcie's hand. "Okay, girl, shall we lead the way?"

Dulcie skipped along beside her as the path narrowed and headed upward. A few minutes later, Lynn looked down at her, the little cheeks flushed, mouth set. "Hey, how would you like a piggyback? I love to give piggybacks."

The child nodded, giving Lynn one of her rare, sweet smiles.

"Okay then," she said as she moved her backpack to the front, then effortlessly hoisted Dulcie over her shoulder.

"Are you sure about that?" Gus called from behind them.

"Absolutely!" Lynn called.

"Absolutely!" Dulcie echoed, giggling.

CHAPTER 8

"What a day," Gus said, leaning back against one of the smooth boulders that lined the perimeter of the clearing. "And what a cool spot."

The children played on the grassy area, stopping by from time to time to grab food or drink from the towel Lynn had spread in front of them.

"There are lots of these cool spots in the Valley and, if you haven't yet noticed, most days are spectacular here. Maybe a little rain, but most of the day is beautiful."

"Yeah, that orographic effect is something, isn't it? I'd never heard of it before I came here." He referred to the unusual cloud formation and abundant moisture that had created the extraordinary green valley between two mountain ranges in the Arizona desert.

"Without it, there'd be no organic farm, or not one that produces like Morgan's Run's does."

"We're lucky," he said, reaching forward to brush an errant strand of hair from her forehead. Startled by the intimate gesture, she sat up straight.

"Sorry. Did I overstep?" he said.

"No... It's fine."

She turned her attention to the children, not certain what to say.

They were happily playing in the grass, weaving flowers, weeds, and sticks.

"Guess I don't have to state the obvious. As you can see, I'm pretty rusty at this. I've never really dated. Lissie and I were together so long."

Lynn smiled. "You're not so bad."

He grinned, a genuine smile that lit up his handsome features. "Good to know."

"So is this a date?" she asked, eyes mischievous.

"Let's call it a pre-date."

"So?"

"So, in case it's not apparent, I'd like to get to know you better, Lynn. I'm aware that I carry considerable baggage, so I will completely understand if you're not interested. In fact, I've been interested...attracted to you...since I first brought the kids to the Cottage, but I decided you were *way* out of my league."

"Oh?"

"Way smarter for one."

She chuckled. "I very much doubt that."

"I mean, I'm not a complete dunce. I did go to college. Degree's in animal husbandry. Kind of fell into the horse training when I came back home."

"From what I hear, you're really good at it."

"It suits me." At that moment, he spied Cal climbing a boulder. "Dulcie, get him down, will you, sweetie!" he called as he jogged across the clearing. By the time he reached them, Dulcie had managed to wrestle her brother down and divert his attention to their pile of sticks and grass.

Gus turned around and came back, sitting down. "So...where were we?"

Lynn smiled. "Your profession and how it suits you."

"Yeah, I really know how to woo a girl, don't I? Anyway, before my son loses it and we have to head back, I was wondering if you might like to go on an actual date sometime? Dinner? Lunch? Whatever works for you?"

"I'd love to," she said, placing her hand over his.

Gus curled his rough fingers round hers. "That's great. I'll work on a sitter."

"Except for the big clambake tonight and the wedding next weekend, I'm pretty free," she said.

"No other hot dates on the calendar?" he asked, adding, "Though of course, that's none of my goddamn business."

"Not at the moment. I believe Cal the chimpanzee is at it again."

"Yup. We better get packed up. It's almost nap time for him, and he'll need it before tonight's party."

Lynn pulled her backpack out after her in the condo lot. "Thanks, guys," she said, smiling at the kids, then Gus. "I'll see you three at the farm for the big party, right?"

"Right!" Dulcie said as Cal's head nodded to the side.

Gus cringed. "Uh-oh, we better get a move on so he doesn't fall asleep in the car. Will be hell to pay later. See you soon."

"You bet," Lynn said, her heart lighter than it had been in many years. *A kind, handsome, steady man has asked me out. Almost a miracle!*

CHAPTER 9

Lynn pulled her Toyota SUV onto the grassy lot at Valley Stables, mouth agape at the sight in front of her. A huge blue-and-white-striped tent stood in the open field, with several smaller tents to either side. Smoke billowed from two burlap-covered mounds to the north, and several people in aprons stood around each mound.

"Hey, Lynn!" Beth Morgan called as she and Lang hopped out of his Rover, Lily in his arms.

"Hi, guys, hi, Lily! This is incredible, isn't it?"

"Spark and Dad are like two pigs in shit," Beth said.

"Whose idea was this, anyway?" Lynn asked.

"Oh, that's right. The invitation didn't say. It's Buck's birthday. Not a milestone or anything. I think he's turning thirty-two, but apparently, he's always wanted a clambake birthday."

Lang chuckled. "And he has the father to make it happen."

"Your parents are no slouches either. Oops, sorry, that just slipped out. No offense intended."

"None taken," he said. "My folks are comfortable, but they'll never be in Spark's league, or the Morgans', for that matter."

Lang's parents owned the successful Saguaro Vineyards just south of Morgan's Run, and they also raised prize Angus cattle.

"Few are," his wife said, and speak of the devil, our hosts await us. Hi, Mom, Dad, Spark!"

Beth hugged her parents and Spark, then Lynn and Lang greeted them. Standing beside Leonora was a tall, lanky, slightly younger man with shaggy eyebrows and thick salt-and-pepper hair. He bore a remarkable resemblance to Ben Senior. Lynn smiled as she extended her hand. "You must be the recently arrived uncle."

"Oh, mercy, where are my manners," Leonora said. "Lynn, this is Ben's brother, Richard. Dickie, Lynn runs our wonderful ranch day care center."

"Pleased to meet you," he said with a killer smile, his grip firm.

Another Morgan charmer, she thought. "So nice to meet another member of this incredible family."

"A long-lost one," Leonora said, patting Richard's shoulder. "But we're going to change that."

"Doesn't my sister-in-law look beautiful tonight?" he asked, arm circling Leonora's shoulders. And she did. Not a strand of her shoulder-length blonde hair out of place, Leonora wore dressy faded jeans, a blue beaded jersey, and espadrilles with chunky heels. Sparkling silver earrings and bracelets completed the simple, elegant ensemble.

Lynn nodded. "Sure does. Always."

"You look lovely too, dear," Leonora said. "Love that top. Gabriela's?"

"I wish," Lynn said, chuckling. "No, I got this at SD," she said, referring to Saguaro Dreams, a three-story emporium in town that sold a little bit of everything.

"I've got to get in there!" Leonora said, turning to greet new arrivals. "Have fun, dear ones!"

Lynn wandered off, eyes scanning the room, relieved to spy Polly and Kevin near one of the bars. As she headed toward them, Maggie and Ben Morgan waved hello. Little Bennie was already off rolling on the grass outside the tent with Jasper and Ruthie Morgan. Baby Charlotte crawled around at the side of the melee, her father watching her.

"Some things never change," Ben said, one arm around Maggie, the other around Emma. "My sister hasn't gotten the memo that she's an adult and has a kid."

Maggie smiled. "Thank goodness. I hope she never does. Hey, Em, there's Toby," she said as Jeb and Amy Barnes came in, pushing their son's wheelchair. Emma ran off to greet them, and Lynn excused herself and headed for Polly, now standing alone.

"Hey, partner, where'd your husband go?" she asked, hugging her friend.

"He's checking on Jasper. No telling what those two'll get into at a clambake, no less! Do you believe the smells out here in the middle of the desert? Feels like we're home in New England, doesn't it?"

"No clambake at home ever had such a concentration of gorgeous cowboys in one place."

Polly laughed. "And two of the Morgan boys aren't even home yet!" Sam and his wife, Rose Dillon, Lang's sister, lived in Maryland, and Kyle Morgan and his fiancée, Harriet Winthrop, in Massachusetts.

"Let's not forget your hunky guy, and he's not even a cowboy," Lynn said.

"Nor yours," Polly said, eyes dancing with mischief.

"There's no 'yours,' thank you very much."

"Oh, I beg to differ. And here he comes now."

Lynn followed Polly's gaze, and sure enough, Gus was headed their way, Cal in his arms, wriggling to get down, Dulcie at his side, grasping his belt. He did look pretty hunky in jeans, running shoes, and a faded work shirt, sleeves rolled up to reveal strong, tanned forearms.

"Stop it," she said, poking Polly as she smiled at Gus and Dulcie. "Hi, guys!"

"Hi, Lynn, Polly," he said, smiling warmly.

"Hi, Dulcie!" Emma Morgan called as she wheeled Toby to join them. "Wanta come with Toby and me? We're going out to play with Aunt Ruthie. Cal can come too, Mr. Casey. I'll watch him."

"You sure?"

The Morgans' mature nine-year-old beamed at him. "Yup! Toby'll help me."

Toby Barnes held out his arms, and Gus placed his son on his lap. "Thanks, guys. If you need help, just shout."

Cal knew Toby well from after care at the Cottage, and he immediately put his arm round him, bouncing up and down. The women and Gus watched the group heading out, and Gus shook his head. "Not sure how long it'll last."

"But enjoy it while it does. If I know Emma, she'll keep them busy for a long while," Polly said. "Excuse me, you two. Must make a stop in one of Spark's fancy Porta Johns."

You stinker, Lynn thought, knowing full well that Polly probably didn't need a bathroom break any more than she did. "Subtlety has never been Polly's forte."

"Oh?"

"She thinks we should be alone."

He laughed. "I love Polly."

"Hmm…"

"What about tomorrow night?"

"Excuse me?"

"I know it's a school night, so we could do something early. Willow's friend Peggy is free to sit."

"You move fast," she said, meeting his green eyes. *I could get lost in those eyes in no time flat.*

"The way you look tonight, I'd better. Every guy in the place'll be after you."

"That I doubt," she said, pleased that she'd taken time to choose her outfit. She wore black jeans that hugged every curve, strappy sandals, and a silky floral tee, its vee neck revealing a hint of cleavage. Her hair hung loose, falling over her shoulders, but she'd brought a scrunchy to tie it back during the meal. "And wait till you see me after dinner. I love clams, so I'll be a hot mess of grease and broth."

"Sounds okay to me."

"Yes."

"Excuse me?"

"Yes, I'd love to have dinner tomorrow night."

She was rewarded by a huge, shit-eating grin. "Great, terrific. Pick you up around seven?"

"Perfect."

"Can I get you a drink?"

"I'd love a beer, thanks."

"What about Polly?"

"She'd probably love one too. Thanks, Gus."

As he headed for the bar, Polly returned. "How's it goin'?"

"Never mind how it's goin'! You're about as subtle as a sledgehammer."

"Oh pooh. Someone's gotta give you two a nudge."

"No, they don't. By the way, I ordered you a beer since I assume you're not telling anyone yet. You can pretend to drink it, then hand it off to Kev."

"Good thinking. No, we're not telling anyone. I have a doctor's appointment next Tuesday. We'll see after that."

"How are you feeling?"

"Pretty good, actually. So? Are you dating or what?"

"Dinner tomorrow night. Dinner, that's all."

Polly clapped her hands. "I knew it!"

"Knew what?"

"Lynn Manguilli, for a smart woman, you really are clueless. A man doesn't look at someone like Gus Casey looks at you if he's not head over heels."

"Don't be ridiculous!"

"We'll talk again after tomorrow night," Polly whispered. "Here comes Mr. Bedroom Eyes now."

"Here you go, ladies," Gus said. "Desert Amber drafts from one of the kegs. The birthday boy tapped a new keg just for you. He's excited" They spied Buck Foster behind the bar grinning like the Cheshire Cat. Not a cowboy, but a very attractive, self-assured West Coast artist; speculation abounded every time he visited about why the very eligible bachelor was still unattached.

"Thanks, Gus," Polly said. "I'd better head out and assist my poor husband. Jasper really is a handful."

"I better follow Polly," Gus said, "although I will be sorry to leave your side."

"I could always tag along?"

"I was hoping you'd say that." He placed a hand on the small of her back. "Shall we?"

Lynn moved forward on shaky legs, his touch enough to send shivers of sensation from her head to her toes. *It's been much too long since I've been with a man,* she reflected as they walked side by side, Gus's hand still resting on her back.

CHAPTER 10

"I warned you not to sit near me," Lynn said as Gus eyed the enormous pile of clam shells in front of her.

"You really do like clams, don't you?" he said.

"My favorite food in the world." She nodded to the server, who filled the clam bowl in front of her, then plunked a lobster onto her plate. "I never would have believed they could taste this good coming all the way from Maine."

"On Spark's private plane, no less," Kevin said. He, Polly, and Jasper sat across from Lynn, Gus and his kids, Maggie and Ben Morgan beside them with Bennie. Emma was sitting with her grandparents and Toby at the head table.

"Well, there is that," Lynn said, cracking her lobster, explaining the process to Gus. He hadn't been terribly fond of the steamers, but had enjoyed the rest of the bake—sausages, hotdogs, onions, corn, and two kinds of potatoes. He was also quite keen on the chowder and clam cakes that had preceded the main meal.

After Gus fumbled with the lobster crackers for several minutes, he seemed to get the hang of it, and when he took his first bite of succulent meat dripping with butter, he sighed. "Incredible."

Ben Morgan waved a lobster claw at him. "And there's plenty more where that came from."

Lynn had come prepared with a dish towel and a can of wet wipes. As the meal concluded and ice cream was served in cups and cones, she managed to get most of the grease from her hands and arms, but despite wearing a lobster bib, her shirt was dotted with stains.

"Told you I'd be a hot mess," she said to Gus, who was eyeing her.

"You look beautiful," he said quietly.

She looked up and found his eyes soft. "You're a good man, Gus Casey."

"Not sure you'd agree if you knew what I'm thinking at this moment."

"Oh?"

"Better left for a time when we're alone."

"Then I'll ask again sometime," she said, her voice sultry.

"I sure hope so."

At that moment, Cal began screaming, and they didn't have another moment alone for the rest of the evening. *No matter,* Lynn thought as she drove home later. *That moment said it all and more!*

CHAPTER 11

Lynn dressed carefully for her dinner with Gus, choosing a blouse she knew flattered her figure and brought out the flame in her dark eyes. Its neck plunged to a tantalizing vee *with just enough cleavage to get Gus' attention*, she mused, brushing her thick hair till it fell languidly over her shoulders. She wore silver at her neck, ears, and wrists, black skinny jeans, and strappy sandals. "I'm never gonna be Twiggy, but I look okay," she said aloud, applying a spritz of Opium, a gift from her mother.

"If you're going to wear perfume, you might as well knock 'em for a loop," was Sorcha Manguilli's motto. Lynn gazed at the photo of her parents on her dresser. She missed them and resolved that before the summer was over, she'd take a few days and go home. They'd talked about closing the Cottage for two weeks in August, so that would work perfectly.

The doorbell rang, and she grabbed a shawl, which she draped over her shoulders. When she threw open the door, she knew by Gus's expression that her outfit hit the mark.

"Wow, you look sensational," he said.

"Thanks, you look pretty good yourself," she replied. And he did, in a blue sport shirt and khakis. For once, his unruly hair looked tamed, and she wondered how he'd accomplished that and gotten the kids settled with a sitter and all. "Am I okay? I mean, I'm not that dressy. We're not going somewhere fancy, are we?"

"Vermillion. Kevin recommended it. Is that okay with you? Do you know it?" He referred to a popular farm-to-table restaurant south of town.

Lynn smiled. "It's great and not fancy."

He offered her his arm. "Shall we?"

As she grasped his forearm, Lynn felt her temperature rise. When she let go and slipped into the cab of the truck, she realized she'd been holding her breath and let it out with a whoosh. They drove out of town chatting about their day and how the kids had taken to Peggy, the sitter. Safe topics that skirted around the palpable attraction that crackled between them.

After parking, he hopped out and came around to open her door, extending his hand.

It was twilight and the farmland surrounding them was fading along with the light. Before she knew what was happening, Gus drew her close and kissed her, his hand at the small of her back. His lips were soft, inviting. Startled, Lynn responded as her knees threatened to buckle. Their tongues entwined, and the kiss deepened, their bodies pressed against each other. Just as she felt his arousal against her tummy, the lights of another car came down the drive. "Oh, oh," she sputtered.

Gus released her, his hand cupping her chin, eyes searching hers. "Too much?"

"A surprise."

"I didn't think I could wait until after dinner to kiss you. Not the way you look tonight."

"I'm glad," she said. "But we better stop now. I don't think they rent rooms by the hour."

"Too bad," he said, taking her hand as they walked toward the door of the restaurant.

Later, as they sipped Saguaro Winery's crisp white sauvignon blanc, Lynn smiled at him. "No beer tonight?"

"Tryin' to rise above clodhopper."

"Well, you made a good choice. This is one of the Dillons' finest."

"Is there anything this Valley doesn't grow or produce?"

"Clams, lobster, and you and me," she said brightly. Sitting in the soft glow of Vermillion's interior, she realized she was happy, really happy. *Please let this feeling last beyond tonight.*

"Everything okay?" he asked as Edna Loggins, the owner, stopped by the table.

The round-faced, cheerful owner, tray in hand, smiled from one to the other. "Good evenin', folks. Sorry I wasn't here to greet you. Is Nancy taking good care of you?"

"She is, indeed," Gus said, "and I certainly see the family resemblance."

"Yes, she inherited my cheeks, poor girl. Can I help with menu selections? The chef's specials tonight are getting good reviews so far."

"I was thinking of the trout," Gus said.

"Excellent choice. And you, dear?" she asked, turning to Lynn.

"I thought the pork kebabs sounded amazing."

"They are. Our own pigs, humanely grown and slaughtered. And most of the vegetables are from Morgan's Run tonight. Take your time. I'll send Nancy in a few minutes in case you have questions. Your first time at Vermillion?"

Gus nodded.

"Then appetizers are on the house. Just tell Nancy what you'd like. Enjoy."

Gus grinned as Edna disappeared. "We're in the Valley, aren't we?"

"Sure are."

"Amazing. Anyway, getting back to you and your thoughts a few minutes ago?" he said.

Lynn laughed. "What with thinking about just which luscious appetizer I'll order, my thoughts, whatever they were, have flown out of my head."

"Honest?"

"No," she said, softly. "Honestly, I was thinking how happy I was and am right now and wondering how long it will last."

"Forever, I hope."

"Of course, it might have something to do with the wine and that kiss, but I am happy to be here with you. Just admitting that's a major step for me. I'm usually pretty guarded with men."

He reached over and took her hand. "I'm happy too. I was going to say thanks for coming out with me, but I knew you'd get after me."

Lynn gave him a coy look, then turned to her menu. "Yes, I would. Now here comes Nancy to take our order. I'm going to have the bruschetta. How 'bout you?"

They chatted amiably throughout the delicious meal. Edna suggested that they take their dessert sampler and coffee on the porch, which they did. The night was warm and clear. Stars blanketed the sky as the crescent moon rose. Lynn sighed, leaning back on the soft cushions of the wicker love seat. "This is heaven."

Gus sat beside her, the tray of coffee and dessert in front of them. "Yes, it is." He took her hand and began massaging her palm, sending shivers of sensation through her.

"Hmm... That's nice," she murmured, leaning back, closing her eyes.

"You're a beautiful, amazing woman, Lynn Manguilli."

She opened her eyes and gazed over at him. "Thank you. You're pretty special yourself, Mr. Casey."

"No, I'm not, but thanks for saying so. I'm kind of a country bumpkin. I don't have much experience with matters of the heart, never mind sex."

Lynn reached over and traced a line along his jaw. "Confession. I may seem worldly, but I'm not. I've only had a few boyfriends in my twenty-nine years, and none of them lasted long."

"I don't believe that," he said, leaning over and kissing her lightly. "I'm gonna restrain myself 'cause we're technically in the restaurant, but I would sure love to take this further."

"Maybe we should take the desserts to go?" she murmured. "We can enjoy them and coffee at my place, if you don't have to get back too soon to relieve Peggy?"

"Great idea," he said, standing. "I'll just find Nancy or Edna and settle up."

CHAPTER 12

They held hands on the ride north to town. Gus's caressing fingers drove her crazy with white-hot heat. Inside the condo, the dessert container dropped to the floor as the door closed and they found each other. Clothes flew as they moved toward the bedroom.

"It's this way," she said, breathlessly as Gus's kisses trailed down her neck. He had slipped her blouse over her head and was now cupping her full, round breasts, fingers slipping under the lace to tease her nipples to hard, tight knots of sensation. In a blur of desire, Lynn felt his hardness against her and reached down to stroke him as she undid his belt, then pants to release him.

Gus groaned as her hand found flesh and she began caressing, stroking, and massaging. "Oh sweet Jesus," he said. "Lemme get out of these pants and get you out of these."

She grinned. "They're skinny jeans, so they're plastered on. Here, let me help you." She stepped back, slipping the jeans down slowly, her panties following. She stood for an instant in her bra and nothing else until he pulled her into his arms again, lifting her, swinging them both onto the bed. He held something in his left hand, which he set on the table. "Condom," he said. "Only if you're okay taking this further?"

"What do you think?" she asked, unhooking her bra, releasing her full, glorious breasts.

He whistled. "Beautiful. I knew they'd be beautiful, but boy, this is beyond my wildest imagination." He leaned forward, taking one, then the other breast in his mouth, his lips and tongue teasing and suckling until Lynn cried out at the crest of a blinding orgasm.

He reached between her legs, fingers gently probing until they reached her warm, wet depths. "Oh baby, tell me what you want, and I'm yours," he said, voice husky as his fingers stroked and thrust in and out.

"Condom now," she whispered, kissing his shoulder. "Take me now, please."

"My girl, I thought you'd never ask," he said, slipping the condom on, body poised above her, his lips everywhere on her mouth, neck, breasts. Lynn stroked as she guided him closer, opening herself and drawing him in. As Gus thrust down, she rose to meet him. In a frenzy of longing, their bodies craved one another, couldn't get enough. Closer and closer, deeper and deeper.

"Oh Gus!" she cried. "Please, please, please!"

Concerned, he gazed down. "You okay?"

"More than okay. Please don't stop. Don't ever stop!"

In tandem, their bodies came together again and again, until they peaked in a dizzying crescendo of sensation that left them hot and slick on the cool sheets of her bed. "Oh, my darling girl," he said huskily. "I have to risk it this one time and say thank you, thank you. That was incredible." He kissed her eyelids, nose, and mouth. Soft kisses that touched her core.

Lynn moved so she could gaze into his eyes. "Thank you, Mr. Casey. For a country bumpkin, that was amazing."

He grinned. "We try."

Side by side, Gus still deep inside her, they held each other tenderly. "Wish I could stay here all night," he whispered.

"Me too. Want that coffee now?"

He smiled. "Not especially. You?"

"Not as much as this," she said, moving against him, hips circling, caressing him.

"You think so?"

"I know so," she said, smiling, her lips moving down his neck to his chest. She could feel him growing inside her as she continued her slow, rhythmic hip dance. "Hmm... Someone's interested."

"You betcha," he said, interrupting her sensual movements to ram into her warm, moist depths. Instantly, he pulled back. "Too much?"

"Never," she murmured as she continued to circle, thrust, circle, thrust, until they were both panting, rutting, and making love to each other as if their lives depended on it.

When the climax came, they sank gratefully into each other's arms and lay still and sated. Finally, Gus said, "That was indescribable. I've been married, had two kids, and never experienced anything like that."

"Me neither," Lynn said softly. "Me neither."

They lay entwined for some time, until he stirred. "Hey, beautiful girl. I'd gladly stay like this forever, but real life calls." They kissed deeply, with lots of tongue, then he groaned, slowly slipping out of her.

Gus padded through the condo gathering his clothes and dressed quickly. Lynn followed, wrapped in a purple silk bathrobe. When he shrugged into his jacket, he turned back to take her in his arms. "This was a sensational night for me. Can we do it again soon?"

"I'd like that," she said, kissing him.

"You look really sexy in that robe."

She gave him a shy smile. "Thanks. Drive safe." And then he was gone, the cool night air taking his place as the door opened and closed. Lynn hugged herself, then picked up the discarded takeout box and popped it into the fridge.

Not sure where this is going, she thought, turning off the lights, *but I'll gladly go along for the ride.*

CHAPTER 13

"So?" Polly said, greeting her the next morning. "How was it?"

Lynn sighed. "Wonderful. Almost like a dream."

"Ooh, that sounds *very* promising and definitely more than dinner! Tell me more."

Lynn related the highlights of their dinner at Vermillion and afterward until they were interrupted by the rush of children and the start of the day. Christy Perez arrived first, Jasper and Kevin at her heels, then Ruthie and Lang dropped off Charlotte and Lily. Willow scooped up the little ones and headed for the quiet play area as Jasper ran by, headed for the blocks. As the two directors moved about the rooms, Polly gave Lynn sly winks and encouraging pats on the shoulder.

The day was in full swing and they were laying out craft materials when Polly looked around. "Gus is late today."

"Is he?" Lynn asked, willing her voice to sound nonchalant. Dulcie and Cal were usually the first to arrive. Her cell phone buzzed, and she grabbed it. "Hello?"

"Hey, it's me."

"Yes, hello. Good morning," Lynn said, nodding as Maggie stepped in with Bennie and Emma.

"Dulcie's sick. Woke up in the night with a fever. I'm gonna stay home with her, and I'll keep Cal too."

"I'm sorry, poor baby," Lynn said. "Tell her we'll miss her and to get better soon."

"Lynn?"

"Yes?"

"I had a great time last night."

She smiled. "Me too. Anything we can do for you?"

"I'm all set. Just talked to my sister, Laurie. She was planning to come in a couple of weeks, but she's gonna try to switch and come earlier. Be good for the kids and me."

"Of course. Take care," she said, ringing off.

"You okay?" Maggie asked as she hung up Ben's things. "You look like you've had some bad news."

"No, all's well. Just a sick child. Dulcie Casey."

"Oh dear, hope she feels better," Maggie said. "I'm going to run, but I wanted to warn you. My mother-in-law's coming to get Emma, and she's bringing an entourage for a quick tour of the Cottage, ranch, and town. Hope they're not too disruptive."

"Oh?" Polly said, looking up from her task.

"Helen Winthrop arrived last night and she brought her daughter, Lucy. I believe they will be accompanied by Weezie Morgan, Ben's cousin. You met my Uncle Dick, didn't you?"

Lynn and Polly nodded.

"Weezie's here for the wedding along with her brother, Wolfie, who I do not believe will be joining this morning's marathon tour. Heaven help us. I hope they don't drive you crazy."

Lynn smiled. "No worries. We'll be fine. Have a great day."

With a kiss to her daughter and son, Maggie Morgan hurried out, waving over her shoulder. "Remember, they're meant to have a quick visit. I told Emma to hurry them along 'cause she doesn't want to be late for school."

Popsicle-stick puppet making had just begun when Leonora Morgan swept in with three other women. Emma had been helping Christy apply eyes to her puppet, but she hopped up and came to greet her grandmother and Helen, whom she hadn't seen since the older woman's previous visit six months earlier. "Hi, Gran, hi, Helen," she called, hugging them each in turn.

"Good morning, Precious," Leonora said, kissing the top of her head. "This is Lucy, Helen's daughter, and your cousin Weezie. Can you say hello? Bennie, you too." She pointed to her grandson, whose tongue stuck out the side of his mouth while he was engrossed in his puppet construction. "That is Ben the third. Takes after his father and uncles."

Leonora swept around, introducing everyone and giving Weezie and Lucy a quick tour of the Cottage while Helen stayed with Lynn, Polly, and the others, helping with the craft project.

"What a wonderful school," Lucy said as they stepped back into the room. She was tall and slender like her mother, athletic, her brown hair cut in a bob, pulled back with a tortoiseshell headband. "I wish I'd had something like this when my kids were tiny."

Lynn watched her blue eyes scan the room, detecting a sadness in their depths. She guessed Lucy to be a bit older, but it was hard to judge age some times. On the other hand, Weezie had to be early twenties, her dark brown hair cut short, a stylish pixie that suited the petite young Morgan, her chocolate eyes dancing with light. She had a perfect figure and was dressed casually in capris and a scooped, sleeveless top, a light sweater thrown over her slim shoulders. Beauty ran in the Morgan family, and this young woman was no exception.

"Ladies, Lucy runs a very successful children's book business, so she'd be a great resource for you."

"Oh?" Lynn said.

When Lucy smiled, her nose crinkled. "I run the children's room at our local bookstore, and my partner and I have a mail order children's book company."

"What's the name?" Polly asked.

"Merlin's Closet."

"I love that catalogue," Polly said. "We haven't gotten it out here, but I often used to order from you for my nieces and nephews. My sister Kitty'll go crazy when I tell her I've met you. She loves your stuff, especially the adult mysteries you recommend."

"That's my partner's bailiwick," Lucy said.

"Well, she picks really wonderful books. Kitty started the Burren mysteries by that wonderful Irish writer that you recommended. She passed them on to me, and I'm hooked. On book eleven. They're fantastic."

"So glad. I'll tell her."

Weezie Morgan interrupted with "This is totally awesome!" She plunked down next to Lily Dillon, making a silly face that elicited a giggle from Beth and Lang's pretty child.

"Well, ladies, onward we must go," Leonora said. "Can't have Emma late for school."

"Enjoy the tour," Lynn said, rising to help Emma with her things. "Are you going out to Valley Stables too?"

"Already took that tour," Weezie said, "but I'll go back any time. Never seen so many gorgeous guys in one place."

Lynn smiled. "That's the Valley for you."

"Guy I met was from Wyoming, a recent recruit," Weezie whispered. "I could eat him up with a spoon."

Leonora rolled her eyes. "You must mean Gus Casey. He is a sweetheart, but perhaps a bit old for you, dear. There'll be lots of young men at the wedding."

"I don't know," Weezie said, winking at Lynn and Polly. "I think I'm ready to give my heart to cutie-pie Gus."

"Come along, ladies. Time to scoot." Leonora kissed her grandson and hustled the group out the door.

Lynn said nothing until she and Polly were alone in the kitchen preparing lunch. "Cutie-pie Gus indeed! How can I compete with that?"

Polly waved her hand. "She was just showing off. Women like her just like to talk a good game. Gus won't give her a second look. She's definitely not his type."

"And since when did you become an expert on Gus's type?"

"Since I've seen the way he looks at you, dopey!"

"His wife was tiny and petite. Look at me."

"Stop it, Lynn Manguilli! You're gorgeous and perfect, and Gus Casey is hot for you. Forget about cousin Weezie. Besides, she's only here a week, and I guarantee she'll be chasing after every man in the Valley before Robbie and Hope say 'I do' next Saturday."

"Humph," Lynn said, carrying the drinks tray to the dining area where Willow and Rusty had all the children sitting, lunch boxes open. Despite morose thoughts about Weezie Morgan, she grinned. "Will you look at this crew, Poll! They're the best, aren't they?"

I knew it was too good to last, Lynn thought, taking her usual seat beside Ben Morgan the third.

CHAPTER 14

Turned out that Dulcie had the flu, which her brother then caught. By Wednesday, Gus had not succumbed, but he'd missed three days of work. He hired Peggy to come for a half day on Thursday as the kids were still too ill to come back to the Cottage. On his way to work, he phoned Lynn, who was setting up alone. "Hey," she said. "How are the kids?"

"Still sick. I've hired Peggy till two, then she has a class. I feel guilty leaving them, but there's so much going on at the farm."

"Wish we could help. They should be good to go soon, right?"

"I think I told you my sister Laurie's trying to arrange things to come for a week or two now. I'd already cajoled her into coming in August when you guys take your break."

"That's not definite," Lynn said. "We hate to leave parents in the lurch, so we're debating whether to close or have Polly spell me, then vice versa."

"Yeah, well, I promised Dulcie we'd go home to Wyoming to see her grandparents for one of the weeks anyway. So, sorry to interrupt. I just wondered if you might be able to spring free for lunch today. Just quick? I miss you and don't know when the heck I'll see you at this rate."

Surprised, Lynn smiled. "Well, I can ask Polly when she gets in.

We're down three, maybe four today with your two and no Lily and probably no Charlotte. She, Rusty, and Willow could certainly handle things. I'll text you in a bit."

"Great," he said, and they rang off.

Lynn was whistling as the door opened and Christy Perez and her mother, Lorna, stepped in.

"So this was a nice surprise," Lynn said as they sat across from each other in a back booth at Gracie's, the popular diner in the heart of town.

"I told you, I missed you," he said, reaching across to take her hand.

"Missed you too," she said as the tall, gangly owner appeared, a yellow streak of what appeared to be mustard in her wiry gray hair.

"Hey, folks, what can I get you?"

They both ordered the burger of the day—mushroom and swiss on rye with Gracie's special sauce—and iced tea. With a wink, Gracie disappeared, and Maria, the waitress, appeared with their teas.

"So, how are you?" he asked, after Maria left them alone.

"Same ole same ole. It's been a quiet week. How about you?"

"I have to admit to a bit of cabin fever, but it's been nice to spend time with the kids that doesn't involve stuffing breakfast in their mouths and rushing them out the door. If I have to read *The Cat in the Hat* one more time, though, I might go crazy."

Lynn smiled. "Dr. Seuss is great, but that's not one of my favorites. I know, I know, it's a classic, but give me *Horton Hatches the Egg* or *Yertle the Turtle* any day."

"I'll take the kids to the library and look for those this weekend."

"You going to the wedding?"

"Yes, all three of us if the kids are better."

So much lay unspoken between them, but neither knew quite how to begin. Finally, Lynn said, "So, busy morning at the farm?"

"You could say that. We've got a few new horses. One of them,

Stella, a real beauty, is the bosses' best prospect for the circuit. She's a little skittish, though. Mostly okay with Alice Hanley, the jockey they've brought in part-time, but she hasn't taken to any of the other trainers. Only lets me saddle and groom her."

"Another horse whisperer?"

"Hardly, but I was there when she arrived. She's a descendant of the Godolphin Arabian, which is huge in race circles. Can only imagine what they paid for her. The bloodline's kind of disappeared, but descendants of Man o' War and Seabiscuit are nothing to sniff at."

"So were you working with this beauty this morning?"

"And every day. The Morgans have a cousin staying with them who fancies herself to be quite the horsewoman. She wanted to ride Stella, and they okayed it."

"Oh? How'd she do?"

He laughed. "Horse did fine, rider okay. Commands the saddle just fine, but Weezie Morgan's no jockey. She talks a good game, but Alice had to take over to complete the warm-up."

"We met Weezie on her tour with Leonora earlier in the week."

"Yeah, she's a spitfire, isn't she? Been out at the farm every day, chatting up the men."

"Oh?"

"Yup, she cajoled one of my guys to take her out tonight. She had her eye on me, but I pleaded sick kids."

"She's pretty."

"And doesn't she know it?"

Maria set their lunch on the table and asked if they needed anything.

"All set," Lynn said, smiling up at her.

They chatted about the kids, work, and town gossip for the remainder of the meal. Gus insisted upon paying with "On the salary our tycoon bosses pay me, I could buy the whole diner lunch."

"You forget I work for them too," Lynn said. She and Polly were paid higher salaries and benefits than the town's public school teachers. Salaries like theirs were unheard of in day care.

"Someday you can buy me a coffee. Got time for a quick walk?"

"Love to. Gotta walk that burger off."

They headed across the street and up onto a footpath that led into the scrubland at the west end of town. They walked for ten minutes or so until they reached a rise where an outcropping of boulders lay to the south edge of the trail. "This is probably the outer limit for me," Lynn said. "Kids are napping now, but I should head back in half an hour or so."

"Me too," he said, reaching out, taking her waist, and pulling her close.

"What are we doing, Gus?" she asked, pushing back.

"We're getting to know each other, right?"

"Sunday night was a bit more than getting to know each other."

Hands on her hips, he lowered his gaze. "I know. That was a surprise to me."

"A nice surprise, but confusing."

He looked up, meeting her eyes. "I'm sorry. That's the last thing I'd want to do, confuse you. I like you, Lynn. I thought I'd never...after Lissie. And then this. You've opened up a whole new world to me."

"Of?"

"Of passion, lovemaking, sex, whatever that was. It was incredible."

"Incredible good?"

"Of course, incredible good," he said, drawing her closer. "What do you take me for?" He kissed her lightly at first, then, parting her lips, his tongue went deeper.

Lynn laced her arms around his neck and responded, her body pressed against him now, her mind and senses awash with feelings she knew she should check but couldn't. Before she knew it, his hands were everywhere, caressing, squeezing her breasts, his mouth and tongue tracing a line of sensation down her neck to her soft mounds. Deftly, he lifted her T-shirt, unhooked her bra, and took her right breast in his mouth, sucking and teasing the right nipple to hardness before moving to the left. By this time, she was panting, her body arching into him, begging. As he fumbled, unzipping his jeans and slipping on a condom, her capris and panties were cast aside.

Gus lifted her, wrapping her legs around him. "What do you say? Want to try for incredible good again?"

She gazed into his eyes and smiled. "Why not." It was her last rational thought as they came together, arching, thrusting, and moving in synchrony to climax.

As their breathing slowed and became regular, Lynn relaxed, her arms still laced tightly

around his neck. Gus leaned back against the flat outcropping, hands still cradling her round, soft ass. "Mmm..." he sighed, burying his face in her neck. "You are one sweet girl."

Lynn stretched her hands till they lay flat on the rock and pushed back. "This girl needs to get her clothes on before someone comes along this well-traveled path." She kissed him, then placed her hands on his shoulders and gently withdrew.

"Aww..." he groaned.

"Aw nothing. Your reputation would probably morph into 'ride 'em cowboy,' while mine would be in the toilet. I can see the headlines now—*Nursery School Teacher Found Naked and Fucking on the Gila Switchback Trail.*"

"Is that where we are?"

"How the hell do I know," she said, pulling on her jersey and buttoning her capris. "But wherever we are, it's too public for what we've been doing."

"Which is the most exciting thing I've ever done in my life."

She smiled, watching him zip his jeans. "I seriously doubt that."

"I'm a country bumpkin, remember?"

"Hmm..." she said. "And I've gotta go."

They walked hand in hand to the edge of town, where the trail ended. He pulled her behind a tree for a quick kiss. "Thanks for meeting me today. I needed you."

"You're welcome," she said. "Gotta go."

He still held her hand and drew nearer, whispering, "I'll have you all day now. Your scent, I mean."

"That doesn't sound like the sentiments of a country bumpkin," she said wryly.

"Maybe I've caught Valley Fever."

"Hmm..." They had reached her car, and Lynn held the door handle.

"When can I see you again?" he asked, reluctant to let go of her hand.

"If the kids come tomorrow, I'll see you at the Cottage. Otherwise, maybe the wedding? Tell them hi for us. We miss them."

"They miss you too. I hate to leave you, Lynn."

"I know," she said, letting go of his hand to hop into her car. "Save me a dance at the wedding?"

"You betcha," Gus said, grinning as she pulled away.

CHAPTER 15

Friday night's rehearsal dinner at the Morgan's Ranch Lodge was hosted by Hope's mother and her husband, Ralph. Polly and Lynn had offered to help serve, and Carmela joined the Lodge's chef, George Baran, to prepare a Southwest barbecue on the terraces. Hope's brother Tom and her Uncle Randy were assisting with hosting duties, and Tom's wife, Betsy, was one of Hope's bridesmaids. Their son Tom Junior and daughter Sara were also part of the wedding party.

A tray of stuffed mushrooms in hand, Lynn stood on the terrace steps talking to Betsy Seymour. "Your kids have certainly grown up," she said. Tom, Betsy, and their kids had visited for Hope and Robbie's engagement party over a year ago. Betsy's son Tommy, nine, was a junior usher, and his sister, Sara, was seven. Sara had been given the choice of acting as junior bridesmaid or flower girl, and she had chosen the latter.

"Sure have," Betsy said. "Tommy really shot up this year. He'll be taller than me in no time."

Lynn didn't know Hope or her family well, but she liked what she knew of them. Steady, grounded, and warm would be how she'd describe them, unlike the flighty Weezie Morgan, who was currently hanging on the arm of one of Robbie's Sedona friends, Hal Garrard.

Robbie's tall, dark-haired college roommate towered over the petite Morgan cousin, but seemed to be taking her attentions in stride. All evening, Weezie bounced back and forth from Hal to red-haired, freckle-faced Dave Burrows, Robbie's other coworker from Sedona.

Betsy noticed Lynn's gaze. "She's something, isn't she?"

"You could say that," Lynn said. "I'd better keep passing before these mushrooms get cold."

"You and Polly are so kind to be helping tonight."

"Are you kidding? After all this family has done for us? We love it. Have a great evening."

"Yes, and we'll see you at the wedding."

As Lynn passed her tray, she came to the Sedona group. "Hi, Linda," Weezie said. "Do you know Hal and Dave?"

"Hey, Lynn," Dave said, smiling at her. "Good to see you."

"You too," she said, nodding at Hal.

"Oh, my bad," Weezie said. "Thanks, *Lynn*. These mushrooms are to die for."

Lynn headed for the buffet table, where Polly was setting out plates. "Could that woman be any more nauseating?"

Polly giggled. "I'm assuming you're talking about our kissing cousin."

"Ha, ha. What's next anyway?"

"Just a few more passes, then Hope says for us to have dinner. Everyone's out on the terrace. We can eat in here with the staff or join the family."

"I vote staff," Lynn said. "Then we're to pass dessert trays, right?"

"Right."

"Wow, you gals get around," a voice said as Weezie popped up behind them. "Super nice for you to help out this way."

"The Morgans are like family to us," Polly said. "We love helping with Robbie and Hope's special party."

Weezie nodded. "It is quite a family. I'd never met my cousins before."

"They're incredible people, warm, generous, and kind, every one of them. The in-laws too."

"I adore Hope, Lang, Maggie, and Harley. Just met Rose and Harriet."

Lynn smiled. "As you say—quite a family."

"And we'll be living near Kyle and Harriet, so that's really cool," Weezie continued, eyes scanning the room.

"Oh?" Polly said.

"Yup, Dad's just bought a huge parcel of land near Horseshoe Crab Cove. He's moving all his operations from Maine to Massachusetts. Wolfie and I'll be coming with him. Maybe some of the other sibs."

"What're his plans for the property?" Lynn asked.

"Horse breeding, for one. That's why he's so keen on picking their brains out at Valley Stables."

"That'll be great," Polly said. "You can start a Morgan's Run East."

Weezie laughed. "We could, couldn't we? If he dared, Dad would poach Harley and a bunch of their workers to come work for us."

"Not if he valued his life, he wouldn't," Lynn said, gesturing toward the terraces. "I think they're calling you all for dinner."

"You're joining us, aren't you?"

"We'll be around," Lynn said, smiling as Weezie hurried off. "She's guaranteed to drive 'em crazy back in Horseshoe Crab Cove. Wouldn't be surprised to hear that Kyle and Harriet have decided to relocate by the end of the weekend."

"Hush!" Polly said, poking her. "She's just young and enthusiastic. You remember what that was like."

"If I ever acted like that, I sure don't remember. Come on, let's get a plate and head into the kitchen. I want to catch up on the latest gossip from the Spa."

Gus had just tucked the kids into bed when his cell buzzed. He clicked on. "Hey, sis."

"Guess where we are?"

"Home?"

"We're two hours south of Sedona, headed your way."

"What?"

"Yup. Should be there soon."

"You said 'we.' Did you bring your rug rat Sparky?"

"No, even better! Jeannie's with me! She had vacation time, and she's dying to see her niece and nephew. We'll bunk together. You've got plenty of room, right?"

Wrong. A hundred-room mansion wouldn't have adequate space for those two friends. "Sure, the kids'll love to see Jeannie."

"You too, of course."

"Of course."

"So we'll see you soon, big brother."

Jeannie Olsen, Lissie's younger sister, had been Laurie's best friend. They were inseparable. *Both great one at a time, like a steamroller when together. Just what I need,* he thought, heading in to get clean sheets.

As he carried sleeping Dulcie to the twin bed in Cal's room, then set to work putting clean sheets on Dulcie's beds, his mind raced. *What about the wedding? What will Jeannie think of my situation and what will both women say about my new relationship with Lynn? This is your life, buddy,* he told himself, grabbing a beer and sitting to wait for the tornado about to touch down. *Don't let Thelma and Louise derail it for you.*

CHAPTER 16

Saturday dawned clear and beautiful. A billowing white tent festooned with flowers and greenery was visible beyond the terrace of the Big House as Lynn and Polly drove up the Morgans' driveway. "Gonna be a perfect day for Robbie and Hope," Polly said.

"It's rarely not a perfect day around here," Lynn said, parking next to one of the ranch trucks.

"Come in, come in," Leonora Morgan said as she greeted them at the front door. "You ladies are truly our saviors. Carmela's out back, and I'm letting her give all the directions. Even Aria is taking orders from Carm today," she whispered, referring to Spark's chef, Aria Firorelli.

Lynn and Polly headed out to the back terrace, now lined with chairs and decorated with flowers and greens. A beautiful arbor of woven branches had been erected at the far end, where the ceremony would take place.

"Good morning!" Carmela called. "Thanks for coming." She quickly put them to work, and they moved about among a half-dozen ranch staff setting tables, filling coolers, and completing last-minute arrangements for tables and bars.

It was after noon when Leonora announced, "Lunch!" and brought out boxed lunches from the café in town. Everyone sat on the grass chatting as they enjoyed the welcome repast. Kyle and Harriet, who were staying at Spark's, joined them, as did Rose and Sam Morgan, who were staying at her parents' house. "We love Maryland," Rose said to Polly and Lynn, "but wish we lived out here for the baby's sake."

"You're not...?" Polly said.

"I am." She beamed. "Three and a half months. We just told our parents last night."

"Congratulations!" Lynn and Polly said in unison.

"Thanks," Rose said. "Sam and I are pretty excited."

"That we are," he said, his arm circling his wife's slender shoulders. "Now if we can find anywhere as awesome as the Cottage back east, we'll be all set." Dark haired with dark eyes like his brothers, Ben and Kyle, Sam was a taller, slender version of his siblings. Like his brother-in-law, Lang, Sam was a long-distance runner.

"Hey, guys," Kyle said, plopping down.

"Where've you been, brother?" Sam asked. "We were looking for you earlier."

"Went out to the farm to see my buddies," Kyle said, grinning as he leaned back, taking a bite of his sandwich.

"Lots going on out there," Lynn said.

"Yup. The new horses are amazing. Now Uncle Dick's tryin' to start up a similar operation right near us, so it looks like I might end up as a resident vet at a thoroughbred farm after all."

"Where's Harriet?" Polly asked.

"She's talking to Carm in the kitchen. She'll be right out."

"Everything okay?" Sam asked.

"Yeah. Gus Casey, remember him? Tom Jacobi's assistant trainer? He's got some people visiting and was tryin' to beg out of the wedding when I saw him this morning."

"Oh, that's too bad," Sam said.

"No worries, the gang's all coming. You know Mom and Dad. The more the merrier. Harriet wanted to make sure Carm got the memo."

People? Lynn thought. She knew his sister Laurie was expected, but hadn't heard of anyone else coming. "So you convinced him to come and bring his friends?" she said, unable to contain her curiosity.

"Sure did. It's his sister who was here before and some friend of hers. We always need more women at these things with all the cowboys."

Rose smiled, winking at Lynn and Polly.

Later, as the two friends and colleagues drove home, Lynn said, "I have a bad feeling about this new development."

"What development?" Polly said.

"The sister and her friend."

"You remember Laurie? She was nice and great with the kids."

"Yeah, she was fine, but I wasn't dating her brother then."

"Why would she care?"

"I dunno, I just have a feeling."

"Well, I wouldn't worry," Polly sat, patting her knee. "Gus will make things work, I'm sure."

Midafternoon, Lynn showered and dried her hair, applying makeup carefully. She had treated herself to a new dress for the wedding from Gabriela's, a small boutique in town. It had cost almost a week's salary, but as she slipped it on, she decided it was worth every penny. As Lynn was self-conscious about her weight, Gabriela had insisted that this style would be slimming, and she was right. Midnight blue, with tiny off-the-shoulder lacy capped sleeves and plunging lace-trimmed vee neck, the dress hugged every curve, its lacy hem falling to midcalf. The dressmaker had convinced her to purchase matching five-inch midnight-blue heels that showcased her shapely legs. She decided on a simple silver chain around her neck, delicate silver filigree earrings, and a few thin bracelets.

"Not half bad," she said, twirling in front of the mirror. She had pulled her hair back in a French braid to showcase her long, slender neck. "Yes, not bad at all," she added, smiling as she grabbed a matching shawl and clutch purse, also from Gabriela's. Kevin and Polly had offered to pick her up, but she had decided to go on her own. Now she wished she'd taken them up on their offer, even if it meant riding with Jasper. Then she wouldn't have to walk in alone.

As she drove up and parked, she breathed a sigh of relief spying her colleague, her handsome husband, and stepson just hopping out of his truck. They waved, then waited for her.

"Wow!" Polly said as she approached.

Kevin grinned. "She's right, Lynn—wow! Wait'll the cowboys get a load of you!"

Lynn smiled demurely. "Thanks, guys." *Now if one special guy is wowed, I'll be happy.*

CHAPTER 17

Hope and Robbie's was a simple ceremony, officiated by her brother, Tom, who had gotten a one-day permit to perform the wedding. After he pronounced them husband and wife, his beautiful sister and her groom turned radiant and happy faces to the audience that included family, friends, ranch staff, and townspeople. Hope wore a light pink silk gown with plunging vee neck, darts to the chest, a fitted waist, a plunging back, and flared skirt. Her long, sandy hair was free, desert flowers held by silver combs her only adornment.

"Breathtaking, isn't she?" Polly whispered.

"Sure is. Her groom's none too shabby either," Lynn said, watching the blond Morgan son hug his parents and siblings as everyone flocked around the couple to offer congratulations. Robbie, his brothers, and his groomsmen wore simple gray suits. Their pale pink ties matched Hope's dress. The bridesmaids—Beth, Ruthie, Betsy, and Hope's friend from home—were in sage green. The dresses were made locally, and each woman had chosen a style that flattered her figure.

Lynn's eyes scanned the crowd, finally spotting Gus to the far left. She couldn't see his companions, except for the top of Laurie's head. As people headed to the receiving line, she lost sight of him completely. After greeting the bridal party, she and Polly headed for the place cards table to discover where they were seated. Polly found their names and called, "Table Ten, we're together!"

Before she turned from the table, Lynn scanned the list and found that Gus and his group were at Table Fourteen. She breathed deeply, wondering if she dared eat in her dress that fit like a glove. As she followed Polly and Kevin to one of the bars, Spark Foster intercepted them. "Well, don't you ladies put the sun to shame!"

"Hi, Spark," Lynn said, hugging their tall, robust employer. "Another glorious party here in the Valley."

"Don't I know it. Have you gals met Lucy, Helen's daughter?" he asked as the lovely lady herself chatted with Richard Morgan at the edge of the tent.

"Yes, Leonora brought her by the Cottage on the Grand Tour early last week," Lynn said.

Spark winked. "Dickie seems quite taken with her. We've barely seen her this week. He's been squiring her around, monopolizing her every free minute."

"Another Valley romance?" Polly said.

"P'rhaps so. Here comes her beautiful Ma now," he said, beaming. As Helen said hello, his arm circled her shoulders.

"How's your visit going?" Lynn asked.

"Wonderful, as always," the tall, slender Helen replied. Elegant and lovely in a simple gray linen dress, she wore her long salt-and-pepper hair pulled back in a braid that reached her waist. She patted Spark's arm. "There's not a more gracious host than this man."

"You're right about that," Lynn said, smiling.

She liked Helen Winthrop, Leonora's friend who had made several trips to the Valley in recent years. Her last two visits, she had stayed with Spark, and the two had become good friends. Freed from the receiving line, the elder Morgans approached and said their hellos, after which Lynn and Polly excused themselves to find their table.

"I'm gonna go find Kev and make sure Jasper isn't in trouble," Polly said. "You okay to find your way, or do you want to come along?"

"Go," Lynn said, waving her hand. "I'm not helpless, you know."

To her surprise, Valley Stables assistant manager Tom Jacobi appeared at her side as Polly scurried off. "Hey, Lynn, you look... Well, you look amazing."

She blushed. "Thanks. You too."

Harley's right-hand man, Tom, was tall, lean, and, like all Valley men, handsome. When he smiled, the features of his craggy face lit up.

"Another great party, huh?"

"Yes, it's lovely. Robbie and Hope seem really happy."

"They're good people."

"How's things at the farm?" she asked, amazed to be having the longest conversation she'd ever had with Tom. She had pursued him several months earlier, but he'd remained aloof and definitely standoffish.

"Goin' along. How 'bout you? Kids behaving?"

She smiled as Jasper and Bennie ran by using calla lily fronds as weapons. "Always. There are two of our live wires now."

As Lynn watched the boys, she spied Cal chasing after them, trying to keep up. In his wake ran his dad. Gus stopped short when he spied his boss. "Hey, Tom," he said, shaking his hand. He turned, his face registering shock as he recognized her. "Lynn? I didn't... You look so..."

"Amazing, isn't she?" Tom said, studying his assistant trainer with a curious look.

"Sure is," Gus sputtered, one eye following Cal, the other on her. "Sorry," he said finally. "I've gotta catch my son before he runs headlong into the wedding cake."

As Gus ran off, Tom turned to her. "Nice guy, Gus."

She smiled. "Yes, he is."

"Are the rumors true, then?"

"Excuse me?" she said, knowing full well to what he referred.

"Someone said you two are dating."

"A bit."

"Glad to hear it. Couldn't happen to two nicer people," he said as Weezie Morgan bore down on them.

"There you are, Tommy!" she said, grabbing his arm. In a strapless red sheath, she dazzled. "I've been looking all over for you! Hey, Lynn, you look terrific. Can I steal Tommy for a sec?"

"Of course," Lynn said, returning Tom's wink as he allowed himself to be dragged away.

CHAPTER 18

Dinner over, dancing had begun with Robbie and Hope's song, "By Your Side." After that, couples packed the floor. Lynn stood at the edge of the tent, smiling as she watched Polly and Kevin dance, so happy and content. She said a silent prayer that all would go well with Polly's pregnancy and the baby they wanted so dearly. *Babies coming all over,* she thought, wondering if that would ever happen to her.

His voice behind her shoulder startled her. "Would you dance with me?"

She turned to find Gus's hand outstretched. "Sure, why not." She took his hand, instantly comforted by his nearness and warmth.

"I'm a little rusty," he said as he led her onto the dance floor.

"Where have I heard that before," she said, smiling as he pulled her close.

"You look beautiful. You stunned me back there. I couldn't breathe for a minute."

"Is that good?" she asked, pleased and calm as they moved as one to Nat King Cole's "When I Fall in Love." Breathless herself, she could feel his arousal against her.

"More than good. I've missed you."

"I hear you have company."

"Yeah, Laurie got in last night."

"And?"

Before he could speak, a sultry, unfamiliar voice came from behind her. "May I cut in? This was one of my sister's favorite songs, wasn't it, Gus?"

Lynn turned to spy a cute blonde in a slinky green satin cocktail dress and strappy silver heels, her hair pulled back in a loose chignon.

"I'm Jeannie, Gus's sister. May I?"

Shocked, Lynn dropped her arms and stepped back.

The bulge in Gus's pants was not lost on his "sister." She frowned, hands on hips. "Gussie? Aren't you gonna dance with me?"

"Lynn, this is Jeannie, my sister-in-law. She's visiting with Laurie."

"Pleased to meet you," Lynn said, extending her hand, which the blonde ignored.

"Later, hon. Gussie, let's waltz!"

Gus gave Lynn an apologetic look as he allowed his sister-in-law to drag him off. Shaken and confused, Lynn walked to the edge of the dance floor, where Polly joined her. "I sent Kev to find Jasper," she said. "We're leaving soon. I saw that. Rude doesn't begin to describe it."

"Have you met her?"

"No, who is she?"

"I believe she's Gus's wife's sister."

"Well, she seems pretty bitchy to me."

"Come on," Lynn said, still shaken. "I'll help you find Jasper and walk out with you. I've had enough of this."

"Are you sure? I'm certain Gus'll come find you."

"I don't want to be found tonight. Let's go."

"Not before I have a dance," Tom Jacobi said. "May I?" He extended his hand, and Lynn took it. *Why not? Two could play at this game!*

~

As she and Tom danced to "Can't Get Enough," Lynn spied Gus, Cal in his arms, headed for the far door of the tent. Laurie, his sister, held Dulcie by the hand and her friend trailed along in their wake. As he reached the door, Gus turned and gave her a wistful look just as Tom swung her around and she was lost in the sea of dancers. After several turns with Tom, Buck Foster asked her to dance. Spark's son was a mystery to her and most Valley people. Sophisticated and elusive, he slipped in and out on frequent visits to his dad's estate. He had been incredibly helpful and supportive of Harriet Winthrop the previous winter as she dealt with ghosts from her past. His calm urbane presence as he took her hand helped Lynn steady her frayed emotions.

"Rough night?" Buck asked as they danced to Etta James's "At Last."

"Weird, would be more accurate," she said. "This band is really good, isn't it?"

"Yeah, Robbie found 'em. They're regulars in Sedona. You look fantastic, by the way."

"Thanks, it's the dress."

"Don't downplay your beauty, Lynn. So you're not a swizzle stick like so many women today. Thank God. I'll take a full-figured gal any day. Maggie Morgan's a goddess to me, and so are you."

She smiled. "Now I know you're kidding. So what about you? We never hear anything about you and a lady friend."

He shrugged. "They come and go. No one special yet, but I keep hoping."

"Look around us. So many loving couples. It does give one hope that it's possible."

"Good role models," he said as the elder Morgans danced by.

"Sounds like your mom and dad were happy."

He nodded. "Just like Ben and Leonora. It's a hard act to follow."

"Think anything will develop with Helen?"

"Doubt it. They both say 'friends,' and I believe 'em. Sounds like she had a rough marriage, then a few years of happiness with a long-lost love. And Dad always says he's had the love of his life and nothing will ever touch that."

"Looks like Richard... Dickie may be starting something up with Lucy Winthrop," she said as she glimpsed the couple dancing.

"I know, he swooped on her the minute he arrived, or I might have tried my hand. She's an amazing woman."

"What's stopping you? I doubt she and Dick are getting married next week."

He made a face. "Complications. I hate complications. And she lives three thousand miles away."

"What's geography when it's true love."

"Uh-oh, another hopeless romantic."

"Hard not to be around here." Lynn gazed across the dance floor and saw Amy Barnes looking in their direction. "I think your sister may want your attention."

"That's right. I told her and Jeb that I'd take my nephew home. Toby must be getting tired."

"Me too," Lynn said. "Have a good night."

"You have a great night too. You know he's crazy about you, don't you?"

"Excuse me?"

"Casey. He seems to have his head up his ass at the moment, but I know love when I see it."

"Now who's the hopeless romantic?" she said, waving her hand.

"Mark my words. I'll be hearing good news about you guys by the end of the summer, or my love barometer's broken."

Lynn laughed. "You're crazy, Buck Foster. Good night!"

After saying her goodbyes and congratulating Robbie and Hope one more time, Lynn headed for her car, smiling. *Buck Foster's love barometer hasn't come up with the likes of Jeannie Olsen, I'll wager.*

CHAPTER 19

"So glad to be here," Jeannie purred as they strolled up the front walk to the house. Gus had been noticeably silent on the drive home, and he remained so, ignoring her.

"Daddy, can we watch a show?" Dulcie asked as he unlocked the door.

He held Cal in his arms and smiled down at his tiny daughter. "Did you have fun tonight, baby?"

She nodded.

"Good. Let's get you two in the bath, then maybe a quick show."

"Yeah!" she said, dropping his hand and running toward the bathroom.

Laurie watched her brother and saw the pain in his eyes. She had been there through the worst of it after Lissie's death. She had also seen the light in his eyes whenever he looked at Lynn Manguilli. In the months since they'd moved to the Valley, she'd waited for him to make his move, but nothing. It was obvious to her that something had changed. His voice on the phone had been lighter, happier, and when she spied them on the dance floor tonight, she knew her hunch was right. He had finally made his move! *It's about time!* Jeannie's intervention had been predictable, but she'd have a word with her.

Nothing was going to get in the way of Gus and the kids' happiness, *not even my best friend.*

As Jeannie disappeared into their bedroom to change, Laurie spied her brother headed for the kids' room. "Hey, Gus, let us take care of this. You relax, okay?"

He turned and smiled. "You know, that'd be great. Can I ask another favor?"

"Of course."

"Can you put 'em to bed? I need to go out for a bit, okay?"

Laurie gazed at him for a few seconds, then said, "Go! Now, before she comes back. Shoo!"

"Kiss the kids for me, okay?"

"Will do," she whispered as he slipped out the door.

WHEN LYNN PARKED IN THE CONDO LOT, SHE NOTICED A LONE FIGURE crouched against the wall, near her condo's front door. A shiver of fear ran through her until he moved and she recognized Gus's familiar form. She took her time, strolling up to meet him. "Whatcha doing? You trying to give a girl a fright?"

"I was thinking more along the lines of a hug followed by an apology."

"Better," she said, smiling in the shadows. "Want to come in?"

"What do you think?"

She unlocked the door and strolled in, snapping on lights in the hall and kitchen. When they stood facing each other at the kitchen counter, she said, "I think I'll take that hug now."

"Oh Jesus, Lynn, I am so sorry."

She hugged him, then stepped back and sat at the counter. "She's a force, your sister-in-law."

"Yes."

"Is this going to be a problem?"

"She's only here for a couple of weeks, and I'm going to talk to her. Laurie will too. She adored Lissie, worshipped the ground she walked on. Right after she died, Jeannie offered to marry me so she could help with the kids. I thanked her and promptly moved to Saguaro Valley."

"Hmm…I see."

"There's no 'hmm.' I'll handle it, promise." He squeezed her knee affectionately. "You really do look fantastic. I mean, you always look fantastic, but that dress…"

"It cost me a week's salary."

"It was worth it," he said, idly stroking her neck, fingers tracing a line down and under the lacy trip of the vee to stroke the tops of her glorious breasts. "Much as I love it, what I wouldn't give to get you out of it and into bed."

"And this is a problem because…?"

"Because I acted like the biggest wimp back there, and you shouldn't want to have anything more to do with me."

"Oh? And what if your fingers are about to send me into orbit with wanting you?"

"If that's true, you've just made me the happiest man on earth," he said, eyes soft as he gazed into hers.

"Well…" she said, standing and turning her back to him. "This zipper is a little tricky. I might need some help."

"Oh, my sweet girl," he said, kissing the back of her neck, lips trailing down her spine.

"You just discovered my secret sweet spot," she said, arching her neck back against his shoulder. "The base of my neck is my most erogenous zone."

"Oh really?" he said, lips tracing upward, their magic bringing her to an explosive climax that left her weak-kneed and shaking.

Gus slipped off the dress and turned her to face him. "Beautiful," he said, kissing her as he reached round and unhooked her bra, letting it fall to the ground. She stood before him now, naked except for lacy panties and her heels. "You are perfect," he said as her arms circled his neck. With one smooth move, he swept her up and carried her into the bedroom, laying her gently on the bed. Still fully clothed, he knelt over her, sliding her panties down. He parted her legs, and his fingers caressed her thighs, moving to her moist wetness so ready for him. "How do you feel about this? Now?"

"I'm yours to do with me what you want," she whispered. "Please."

"I want to make love to you, Lynn. I mean, *really* make love to you."

Lynn pulled him nearer, opening herself as his tongue replaced fingers between her legs, his strong hands now gripping her buttocks, caressing, massaging, and pulling her closer. As he brought her to a blazing orgasm, she screamed, a primal cry of yearning from her core.

With a goofy smile of contentment, his face slick with her, Gus rested against her tummy. "I did it," he murmured. "And you seemed to like it."

Lynn propped herself up on her elbows. "You never?"

"Never. Lissie wouldn't allow it. Said it was dirty."

"What about you? Did she ever?"

He chuckled. "That was even worse."

Lynn sat, drawing her legs up. "I see you're fully dressed, Mr. Casey. We'll have to do something about that."

Slowly, she peeled off his shirt, trailing kisses down his chest to his taut stomach. Gus barely breathed as she unzipped his pants and slipped them and his boxers off. She knelt over him, smiling. "That's better."

He reached up his arms to hug her, but she gently pushed him down. "My turn."

The look of wonder in his eyes gave her courage. Lynn kissed him lower and lower until she took him in her mouth, licking, sucking, her tongue working magic. Gus watched her until sensations overwhelmed him, and he closed his eyes, groaning as she brought him to a blinding release. "Oh Jesus!" he cried, caressing her head, then her shoulders and neck.

Lynn gazed at him, smiling softly. "I'm no expert, but was it okay for you?"

"Darling girl, if it was any more okay, I'd be dead."

"So, where do we go from here. I certainly don't want to kill you."

As she spoke, her hand gently caressed him, and she watched his arousal grow. "Condom handy, Mr. Casey?"

"You betcha," he said, fumbling for his pants and ripping open the packet.

"Let me." She took it from him and slipped it on, stroking and caressing. Before he could rise, she straddled him, lifting herself, guiding him in, hips languidly circling above him, her movements growing more forceful, more insistent.

Her hair fell over her breasts, and he gently smoothed it back to take one, then the other breast into his mouth, tongue working its magic as she arched her back and rode him, every thrust bringing him deeper.

"Oh, my sweet girl!" he cried, hands gripping her buttocks as they rose to thundering simultaneous orgasms, each gasping for breath, their bodies alive with sensation.

As their ardor subsided, she settled on him, and he rolled so they lay side by side, maintaining their sweet connection. He gazed at her, tears at the corners of his soft green eyes. "I never... That was... There really aren't any words."

Lynn smiled. "Sublime?"

"Doesn't even come close," he said, grinning now.

"Then let's not try to give it a name."

"Agreed," he said, kissing her nose, then capturing her lips for a long, deep kiss.

"Can you stay?" she asked, knowing the answer.

"Wish I could. Maybe someday soon."

Lynn threw a blanket over them, and they lay nestled in perfect contentment. Finally, he spoke. "Hey, I hate to do this, but I'd better get back." As he withdrew from her warmth, he groaned.

"Tongues are wagging back at your place, I'll bet," she said, rising to throw on her robe as he dressed.

"Yeah, well, hopefully they'll be asleep when I get home."

"And maybe there'll be pigs flying over your front door."

He grinned. "Okay, I'm an optimist. When will I see you?"

"Monday morning? With Laurie here, are the kids coming?"

"Probably half days. They have a bunch of adventures planned."

She leaned on the door as he grabbed his jacket and found his keys.

"I have so much I want to say to you, Lynn."

"Later, when it's not the middle of the night."

"Later, then," he said, pulling her close for one long, lingering kiss. "Better go before this gets serious and we're making love right here in the hall."

"Hmm... I like the sound of that."

CHAPTER 20

Monday was very hectic from morning till bedtime. The whole crew—kids, Laurie and Jeannie—were invited to Ruthie and Harley's for supper, so there had been no chance for Gus to talk with his sister-in-law. Laurie had spoken to her, but he knew he had to say something as well. Tuesday evening, as the three worked together to get the kids to bed, he decided *now or never*. He made a plan with Laurie. Once the kids were in bed, she announced she was going to the grocery.

"Now?" Jeannie regarded her quizzically. "We can go in the morning."

"Gotta get a few things for the kids' breakfast," Laurie said, giving Gus a sidelong glance.

"I'll come," Jeannie said, rising from the sofa. "Just let me get my sneakers."

"No, I got this." Laurie grabbed her bag and Gus's keys before Jeannie could protest. She winked at Gus and called, "See ya!" over her shoulder before closing the door behind her.

"What was that about? Talk about weird." Jeannie sat on a kitchen stool watching as Gus packed the next day's lunches. Finally, he stowed both kids' bags and his own in the fridge.

Gus smiled. "Laurie's not very subtle, but I did want a few minutes alone to talk to you."

"Oh?" Her eyes sparkled with curiosity as she curled up on the sofa. He took one of the armchairs opposite her.

"Jeannie, you know I loved Lissie with all my heart."

She nodded.

"And I love you like the kid sister you are. Always have, always will. But that's all it's ever going to be—brother and sister."

"How do you know till we try?"

He gazed at her, eyes dark and serious. "I know, that's all. And we're not going to try. Ever."

She huffed. "It was Lissie's wish that we be together."

"That's not exactly true."

"She told me!"

"To look after me and the kids?"

"Yes."

"Not in a romantic way, but because we're family. Just like Laurie looks after us."

"But it could be more. I know it could."

"No, sweetie, it can't."

"Because of that day care woman?" She spit the words out, crossing her arms over her chest in full-on pout now.

"Let's leave Lynn out of it, okay?"

"If it weren't for her, we might have a chance."

"No, we wouldn't. That's one of the reasons I left Jackson Hole. The kids and I needed a fresh start. I wanted you to find someone too. That someone wasn't and isn't ever gonna be me."

"That's cruel. Well, don't expect me to be nice to that bitch."

"That's enough," he said, rising. "I will not have you talk about Lynn like that around me or the kids."

"You don't control me."

"But I do control what my kids are exposed to. Lynn's their teacher, and they're both very attached to her. I will not have you speaking ill of her in front of them."

"Looks like she's more than their teacher to you!"

"Yes, she is."

"So what are you gonna do?"

"It's complicated at the moment."

"By?"

"By a situation that I can't talk about right now."

Her eyes shone with curiosity, and Jeannie sat up. "Who am I gonna tell?"

He smiled at her. "Your best friend, for one."

"Come on, big brother. I can keep a secret."

Gus chuckled. "I can't tell. Not yet, but I'll let you know when I can. Are we okay?"

"I'm not giving up, you know."

"But you're gonna be nice, right?"

She sprang up and gave him an exaggerated curtsey. "The picture of nicety!"

"Thanks, sis," he said. "I'm heading for bed. Night."

He grabbed his cell and considered phoning Lynn, but then plugged it into its charger and went to wash up. *Not yet. Figure things out first, buddy, before you go screwing everything up.*

"Doctor thinks I'm almost five months along," Polly said Thursday morning as they set up for the day.

"Five months? How could you not have known?"

"You know me, very irregular. I just thought being newly married, moving in with Kev and Jasper, and all the changes of the past few months had thrown me off."

"I guess it's a good thing you didn't notice. No morning sickness, no yucky first few months."

"Well, I did have that stomach bug a few months ago. At least I thought that's what it was."

"What'd he say about the rest?"

"That I'm considered a slightly high-risk pregnancy, but lots of women with VSD do just fine, especially those like me who have had the hole in my heart repaired."

"What does Kevin say?"

"He's worried."

"How 'bout your folks?"

"Haven't told them. I'm gonna call tonight."

"Oh gee. Are you sure about this?"

"As sure as I've been about anything except how much I love Kev and Jaspie. Lynn, we heard the heartbeat. We're already in love with our baby. Here's the first picture. You can't tell the sex, and we asked the doctor not to say yet till we think it over."

Lynn regarded her slender colleague thoughtfully as the door opened and Rusty stepped in. "You're not showing at all," she whispered.

Polly smiled, waving to Rusty. "But my pants are getting tight. Morning, Rusty!"

"Still keeping it quiet?"

"At least until we tell our families. It's such a beautiful morning. Let's send Rusty out with anyone who wants to play outside."

Lynn peered out the windows overlooking the Cottage driveway. "Good idea. I see both the jungle gym warriors getting out of their cars now."

By the time Gus arrived with his two, everyone was out enjoying the sunny morning. Lynn pushed Lily on the swing, and Willow had Charlotte in the baby saucer with the rest of the children all over the place. Lynn and Gus hadn't seen each other except at arrival and dismissal, and a couple of times not even then as Laurie often handled afternoon pick up, Jeannie in tow. Lissie's sister had been cordial but distant, and Lynn decided to leave things alone.

After unpacking Dulcie's and Cal's things, Gus brought them to the playground. "Hey," he said, approaching her.

"Good morning," she said. *He looks fidgety and uncomfortable.* "Something on your mind?"

"I've missed you this week."

"Lots going on. I hear from Harley that it's crazy up at the farm."

"Yup. I was wondering… I mean, if you're free. Would you have dinner with me Saturday night?"

"What about your sisters?"

"They'll babysit."

"Oh?"

"We've both had a talk with Jeannie. She's leaving Monday."

"What'd you have in mind?"

"The Red Mesa?"

"Fancy."

"Or we can go anywhere. You choose."

She smiled. "Red Mesa's fine. I've never been there, and I hear it's amazing."

"Seven?"

"Perfect."

"I'll pick you up. Hey, and Laurie'll grab the kids this afternoon. She's probably gonna do both runs tomorrow 'cause I've gotta drive to Gilbert with Harley."

"Oh? What's in Gilbert?"

"Mustangs."

"They're not racing mustangs, are they?" His nearness was almost painful. Lynn had missed him so much this week her heart hurt. She couldn't even broach the subject with Polly for fear the floodgates would open and she wouldn't be able to stop.

"Not necessarily, but you never know. At the moment, Maggie's convinced her father-in-law and Spark to think about a dual mission for the farm, and Harley's all for it. There's such a huge need for rescuing wild horses."

"Sure is. Uh-oh, I see trouble on the jungle gym," she said, grabbing Lily from the swing. "See you Saturday, then?"

"Great, yes," he said as she hurried off.

CHAPTER 21

"You've got to quit work and come home. Your doctors are all back east!" Phyllis Granger said. At Polly's request, Lynn had accompanied her to the airport to collect her mother. And they were now in Gracie's having a late lunch.

When Polly had informed her parents that she was pregnant, her mother had hopped on the first plane. She had been in the Valley less than two hours, and it had already started.

Polly took a deep breath. "This is my home, Mother. And, as you well know, Dr. Blake is very competent. He knows me and the VSD. He's certainly more up-to-date than the team that treated me in grade school."

"Honey, I'd... We'd feel so much better if you were close by."

"And my husband and son would feel better if I were here. I'm fine. I've got Kevin, Polly, and the entire Valley community looking out for me."

Phyllis shook her head. "Lynn? Help me?"

"I'm sorry, Phyllis, but I agree with Polly. She's got a huge support team here. We'll all be looking after her, and you can come out anytime."

"Well, that goes without saying. I'll plan to come two to three weeks before the birth and stay as long as I'm needed."

Polly gave Lynn a pleading look but said nothing.

"My guest room's always ready for you, Phyllis," Lynn said, patting her hand.

"Thanks, sweetie. That's okay for this visit, but I'll need to be at Polly's when the baby comes."

Polly rolled her eyes. "I'll get the check." She rose and headed for the counter.

Phyllis grabbed Lynn's arm in a death grip. "I'm scared to death. Her dad too. You cannot imagine what we went through with her. Operation after operation, never sure if she'd survive."

"But this is different," Lynn said, taking her hand. "She's healthy, Dr. Blake's monitoring her, and we'll all make sure she takes it easy."

"I hope so. I'll cook supper tonight. What would you like?"

"That's so kind, Phyllis, but I've got plans."

"Oh?"

"Dinner date."

"With a man?"

Lynn nodded, smiling. "Yup, an actual man."

"Oh, honey, tell me all about him!"

"Well, he's a widower with two kids. You may have met him around the time of Polly's wedding? Gus Casey. He's the assistant trainer at the new Valley Stables."

"Medium build, sandy hair, and the most beautiful green eyes?"

"Sounds like him."

"Are you serious?"

Lynn shrugged. "Truthfully, I don't know what we are. There's certainly something going on."

"Widowers are tricky. One minute they're on, the next they're off. Some of my friends have dated widowers. Some with great success, others not so much. Has he gotten over the first wife?"

"Hard to tell."

"Hmm..." Phyllis said, finger tapping her chin.

"Hmm, what?" Polly said, hand on her shoulder. "What are you poking your nose into now, Mother?"

Lynn laughed. "She's trying to make sense of my complicated love life."

"My advice—don't tell her a thing!" Polly said. "Come on, Mama. You can stay at our house tonight, then move to Lynn's tomorrow if she'll have you. That way you can give her the third degree after her hot date."

CHAPTER 22

"This is beautiful," Lynn exclaimed as the waiter ushered them into a walled garden with one table in its center.

So are you, Gus thought, watching her. "Harley suggested it," he said.

"And I hope he gave you a huge bonus to pay for it." Her eyes traveled around the space, white-washed adobe walls covered with vines and hanging flowers. Although it was still light, the wall lanterns had been lit, and they cast a soft glow on the terraced walkways. There appeared to be only two points of access, the door from which they had come that led into the restaurant and two French doors at the opposite side, which were closed, the space behind them shrouded in darkness.

"As I told you last week, the salary Spark and Ben Morgan pay me is ten times what the job's worth. I can afford it. You look really pretty, Lynn."

"Thanks." She smiled, lowering her gaze. She had selected one of her favorite dresses, not new, but flattering. The neck of the soft, loose muslin top revealed just a hint of cleavage. She wore a peasant skirt in shades of blues and golds and low, strappy sandals. Unlike her wedding outfit, this ensemble was her and reflected the relaxed, sensual style she favored. In tan sport jacket, blue shirt, and striped tie, Gus looked handsome and put together. Grounded and steady, she felt protected and cherished in his presence. "You look pretty great yourself, but then you always do."

"Good evening, folks," a voice said from behind. "My name is Oscar. I'll be taking care of you tonight. Anything you want on or off the menu, just say the word. Can I bring you something to drink?"

Gus ordered a Desert Amber and Lynn a white wine. Oscar rattled off the evening's specials, then disappeared. When he had closed the door, Gus turned to her. "We could have ordered a bottle of wine, if you like?"

"This is fine. You like beer, and I don't plan to drink myself under the table."

He smiled. "Well, you can if you want. I'm driving."

They chatted amiably, catching up on the week. He related the highlights of his discussion with Jeannie and assured her that the matter was closed. Lynn was able to assure him that his sister-in-law had been genuinely friendly at Friday's pickup and drop off. "How was Gilbert, by the way?" she asked.

"Interesting, powerful, heart-wrenching. There are hundreds of starving horses that need rescuing."

"Any decisions made?"

"Not yet, but I think they'll decide to do it. Lynn... There's something I need to tell you... I..."

Gus was interrupted by Oscar's appearance to take their orders. She ordered chicken piccata, and he ordered veal. When the waiter closed the door, he cleared his throat.

"Uh-oh, something tells me this isn't going to be good news."

"It's not necessarily good news or bad news, just unexpected. A bump in the road or maybe 'a disturbance in the field.' I like that expression. I read a book with that title once, and it's a wonderful description of the unexpected turns in life, don't you think?"

Growing alarmed with all his hemming and hawing, she finally said, "Gus, what is it?"

"Well... It's something completely unexpected. That's what I'm trying to say. You know Richard Morgan? Dickie?"

"Yes."

"Well, he came for the wedding and all, but I think the real reason for his visit was to reconnect with his brother and learn about Valley Stables."

"Yes, Weezie told us something about him wanting to develop a similar operation back east."

"That's the plan." His eyes were grave as they regarded her, a hint of sadness around the edges.

"Don't tell me you're considering... no, you can't be." Unbidden tears sprang to her eyes, and she brushed them away.

"It's only temporary. They need help with the horses in the start-up phases. Choosing them, acclimating them, beginning the training, training the trainers."

"There have got to be people all over the country who can do that job."

"Dick Morgan's offered me a small fortune if I come for three or four months. He's offered to set up and fully fund a college account for both kids. It's the opportunity of a lifetime."

"And then what? You'll come back here and go back to being an assistant trainer? Like that will ever happen."

"It can and it will. That's the only way Spark and Ben would agree to it. They'll match my salary when I come back 'cause I'll be running the mustang rescue program as well as the other."

"So, have you already said yes, then?"

"No. I wanted to talk it over with you. I haven't told anyone—Laurie, my family, the kids."

"What about the kids?"

"I'm considering asking my folks and Laurie to take them back to Jackson Hole. Just for the time I'm back east. When I get back, the house out at the farm will be finished, and they've offered it to me. It's huge and will be great for the kids."

Lynn swallowed. She realized in that moment that she loved Gus with all her heart. *And now I'm losing him.* "You've got to take it," she heard her voice saying, even though her heart was crying *no, no, no!* "As you say, it's the chance of a lifetime, and it's only three months."

"But what about you, and us? Will you be okay?"

"Gus," she said, reaching across to take his hand. "I've been okay for twenty-nine years on my own. I guess I can handle three months."

"You sure?"

She nodded, afraid to say more for fear she would burst into tears.

"You'll write? We'll call? Maybe you can even visit? You said you might go east in August, right?"

"Here we are, folks," Oscar said, delivering their plates with a flourish. "Can I bring you both another drink?" They both ordered wine, and he disappeared.

Lynn barely tasted her food, which she pronounced "delicious," and Gus picked at his veal, his eyes watching her. Sad, wary eyes. Finally, he said, "I've hurt you, haven't I?"

"No."

"Disappointed you?"

"No."

"I don't have to go."

"Yes, you do. I'll just miss you, that's all."

"As I will you, and the kids."

"Then there's Weezie," she said morosely.

"Weezie? What do you mean?"

"You'll be working *very* closely with Weezie Morgan, won't you?"

"I hadn't even thought about that, but what does it matter?"

"She has the hots for you."

He grinned, reaching over to take her hand. "And every other man within fifty miles. No worries there. My heart already belongs to someone else."

"Oh?"

"I'm crazy about you, Lynn. I would've thought that was obvious."

She smiled, fingers caressing his. "Ah, but is it lust or love?"

"Can't it be both?"

"Time will tell, I guess."

CHAPTER 23

Later, as they sipped excellent cappuccino and shared a warm berry tart, he said, "Are you in a hurry to get back?"

"Not especially. Are you?'"

"Nope. Laurie and Jeannie have given me the night off."

"I'd like to find a ladies' room, though."

"Through the door to the left past the bar," he said, a sly smile on his face.

When she returned, he stood by the table. Something had changed, and she saw that the space beyond the French doors was now lit, its soft light spreading onto the terrace. "Bill's all settled. Shall we?" he asked, holding out his hand.

Lynn took his hand, expecting to be ushered out the way they'd come in. Instead, he guided her in the opposite direction. As they reached the French doors, Gus threw them open to reveal a beautiful bedroom suite, the queen bed covered in lace strewn with rose petals, the room lit by the light of dozens of candles. "What in the world?" she asked, mouth agape.

"Cool, huh? It's part of the inn, secluded and well separated from the restaurant proper, but accessible through this walled garden. It's ours for the night, or as long as we want to stay," he said, guiding her inside and closing the doors behind them.

"Really?"

"Really."

With practiced hands, he slid off her top and cupped her full breasts, kissing her silky skin, its citrusy scent intoxicating. "Here's my girl," he said, burying his face in her chest as Lynn arched her body to meet his lips. It wasn't long before all their clothes lay about them and they stood naked, awed by the sight of one another. Lynn was afraid to breathe lest it all be a dream.

"I hope you know how deep my feelings are for you," he said, capturing her lips as his hands moved everywhere from her neck, down her body, then parting her thighs to probe and tease.

Lynn threw her arms around his neck and whispered, "Take me, now. Rough is fine. I need you inside, filling me, warming me."

He slipped on a condom, then turned her until she lay stomach down on the edge of the bed, her round full buttocks beckoning him. "Are you sure about this?" he asked, standing above her.

"Yes, take me. Take me, hard and deep," she whispered, her voice husky and almost unrecognizable.

"Jesus, Lynn," he said as he crouched and thrust himself into her until he couldn't go any farther. Lynn cried out, and he gasped, "Oh God, have I hurt you?"

"Don't stop, Gus, please. Take me, take me, take me!" she begged, and like a rutting bull, he took her full and deep.

She was screaming with orgasmic pleasure when he finally let go, her body convulsed with sensation, suffused with warmth. After their mutual release, he collapsed on top of her, kissing her neck and shoulders, whispering, "Oh, my girl, my blessed, blessed girl."

A few minutes passed, and he pulled them onto the bed, still inside her, cradling her body against his. "Hmm, that feels good," she whispered moving her hips slowly at first, then more insistently. She smiled as she felt him harden and hoped the condom would hold up as they began a slow, gentler rutting that lasted much longer and ended in a breathless climax, her breasts in his hands, Lynn's hands grasping the bedpost with white-knuckled pleasure.

"You okay?" he asked, once again kissing her neck, sending shivers of sensation through her.

"Very okay, but you're doing it again, Gus Casey."

"With you, I could do it again all night," he said, then wrapped his arms tightly around her. "You cold?"

"Never."

They feel asleep nestled in each other's arms and woke shortly after midnight. "Hey, Lynn," he said, kissing her shoulder.

"I know... Time to go."

"Sorry."

"So am I."

"How long do we have?" she asked before he withdrew.

"They want me next week, if possible."

"Isn't that gonna be hard on the kids?"

"They love Laurie and my folks. They'll be okay."

But I won't, she thought as he slipped out of her, leaving a cold that no matter how hot the day, she would not be able to shake.

CHAPTER 24

"I can't believe it," Beth Morgan said as she stood talking with Maggie, Polly, and Lynn at drop-off Tuesday morning. "My mom told me he's leaving in three days. What a shock! Harley must be livid."

"According to Gus, it was his idea," Lynn said.

Maggie nodded. "Yes, well, in a way, that makes sense. They're sending Stella, one of their prize thoroughbreds, with him. Apparently, she's taken a shine to Weezie, so she and Gus can work together and train her."

Lynn's heart sank at the mention of the Morgan cousin. Gus could say what he wanted about her. Weezie would pursue him relentlessly, she was certain. *Let it go, let it go,* she told herself as the others chatted.

"So after he helps your Uncle Richard get his start, he's definitely coming back?" Polly asked as Ben the third ran by on a hobby horse.

Maggie reached out to grab her son, but he eluded her grasp. "I think there's a lot more cooking with the mustangs than they're telling us. I think your dad and Spark are in negotiations to create a national rescue center at the farm as well as one back east on Uncle Dick's property. Excuse me," she said, stepping into the next room to speak to her son.

"Rusty!" Lynn called. "Let's take 'em out for a bit, okay?"

Their assistant nodded, and he and Willow began herding the troops. Shortly after Maggie and Beth departed, Kevin dropped Jasper and, with a quick kiss to his wife and Jasper, he headed out.

Polly reached over and took her hand. "It's gonna work out for you guys. I know it is."

"I love your optimism, partner, but I think that ship has sailed. It sure was amazing while it lasted."

"He's not sailing off the end of the earth. Just a brief cruise."

"Right into Weezie Morgan's open arms."

"Baloney!"

"We'll see. Let's get the bubbles out, what do you say? Too nice to be inside."

"That's the spirit!" Polly said, grinning. "Bubbles are always the answer!"

"For three-year-olds, maybe," Lynn said, giving her a thumbs-up.

"Are you sure about this, brother?" Laurie asked as they packed the kids' clothes. "I mean, don't get me wrong, Mom and Dad are over the moon about having Dulcie and Cal. Me too, but three or four months... Yikes, that's a lot of time."

"I'll come for long weekends a couple of times a month."

"They're gonna miss you."

"Did I explain the offer I couldn't refuse? Richard Morgan has put five hundred thousand dollars in a college account for the kids. And, he's paying me double the ridiculously inflated salary Spark and Ben Morgan already pay me."

"Yes, but will money make up for losing three or four months, maybe more, of your children's lives?"

"Did you not hear the long weekends part?"

"And there's Lynn."

He stopped shoving clothes into Dulcie's bag and looked up. "Don't start."

"I'm sure she's heartbroken."

"She understands."

"I know this is a stupid question since I've seen you guys together, but do you love her?"

"Yes." *There I've said it, admitted it.*

"Have you told her?"

"No, it's not fair."

"Bullshit."

"I'm not gonna tell her I love her and to wait for me. That's dumb and selfish. Besides, this time'll give us both some breathing room."

"Oh, is that needed?"

"Yes...no... Hell if I know. It is what it is."

"Now you're talking gibberish."

"Just drop it, Laurie, okay? I feel like a big enough shit without you making it worse."

CHAPTER 25

Lynn met Gus at Gracie's for lunch the day before his departure. Neither touched their food, and the conversation was muted. As Gus paid the bill, she waved at Gracie and wandered outside to wait for him. The sun was especially warm, and she leaned against the diner wall, closing her eyes, face to the sky. She stirred as the door opened, and straightened up.

Gus came to her side and took her hand. "Lynn, I—"

"Let's not prolong this," she interrupted, turning to face him. "It's hard enough as it is. Let's just say goodbye and good luck and go our separate ways."

He studied her face, shocked at both her tone and words. "Are you talking about today?"

"Yes," she answered quietly.

"Good, because I would hate to say goodbye for good."

She brought her hand up to trace the outline of his jaw. "Take care of yourself, Gus Casey." *I'll miss you more than I could ever express.*

"Shit," he muttered, shaking his head as he grasped her hand on his chin. "I'm making a huge mistake, aren't I?"

"No," she said softly, her gaze warm. "This is a huge opportunity for you, and for Dulcie's and Cal's futures."

"Then why do I feel like a world-class shit?"

"Because you are a kind, caring man."

"I care very deeply about you, Lynn. I hope you know that."

"I do," she said, smiling. "I'm sorry, but I need to get back. I promised Polly 'cause she's got an appointment."

"So this is it?"

She nodded. "I'm sorry I can't see you off, but I've got Phyllis duty tomorrow." She had promised to take Phyllis Granger to Tucson for a day of shopping to give Kevin and Polly a break from the hovering. Now she was glad of the distraction. "I'll say goodbye to the kids this afternoon. I have some little gifts for them. They're in the car. I'll give them to you, and they can open them on the ride to Jackson."

"That was kind of you," he said.

"I'll... We'll miss them at the Cottage."

"As they will miss you. You've really brought Dulcie out of her shell these past few months. My parents are going to be so excited to see the changes in her and Cal."

They now stood next to her Toyota, and she reached in for a small bag. "Here you go."

He took the bag, set it on the car hood, and took her in his arms, his lips capturing hers in a deep, lingering kiss.

Lynn responded, every fiber of her being yearning for his warmth and his touch. After several minutes, she broke away, stepping back, the tickle of his arousal not escaping her notice. "I have to go."

"I know... I...I will miss you, Lynn," he said, wanting to say *I love you*, but still feeling it was unfair to her. "I hope the summer goes well. If you come east to see your family, maybe we can find a way to meet?"

"I'll let you know," she said, hugging him one last time, then hopping into her car. "Will we see you at pickup, then?"

"Yup." She waved as she pulled out, breathing hard to avoid shedding tears.

~

POLLY TOOK ONE LOOK AT HER AND SAID, "I CAN CANCEL THE appointment. You look like you need to go home and have a few hours to yourself, partner."

"I'm fine," Lynn said. "I'll get cots out for nap."

"Lynn, wait," Polly said, hand on her arm.

"I can't," she said. "Not now." Lynn retreated into the nap space, but not before Polly had seen her tears. She called to Willow and Rusty to take over, and she stepped into the room and closed the door behind her.

"I'm so sorry, dearie," she said, hugging Lynn, who was sobbing now.

"I don't know what I'm going to do," she said. "I was fine, you know? I had a life that I knew how to do. It was predictable and pretty ordinary, but I could handle it. Now he comes along with his 'I'm not good enough for you,' aw-shucks routine and steals it all away."

"Look at everything that's happening this summer. The time'll go by really quickly."

"I have two words for you—Weezie Morgan. He's not coming back, Polly."

"I think you're wrong about that. He doesn't give two hoots about her. He loves *you*."

"Well, if he does, he's keeping it to himself."

Hands on hips, Polly gave her a look. "Did you tell him how you feel?"

"That's different."

"Excuse my language, but bullshit," Polly whispered close to her ear. "You're talking like a crazy person."

Lynn dried her eyes. "You're right. I am crazy. Crazy in love. But you're also right that we have a great summer ahead with all the camp activities."

Polly twirled. "And Spark's barn dances start soon." She referred to the twice-monthly dances Spark hosted in his cavernous barn to which the community was invited.

"Yes, there are those to look forward to. Thanks, Poll, for always being such a dear friend."

"The feeling is mutual," Polly said. "What do you say we take the kids outside before nap? It's such a beautiful day."

"I'm right behind you," Lynn said, following her.

LYNN'S HEART SANK AS SHE SPIED LAURIE CASEY PULL IN THAT afternoon. Her expression was not lost on Gus's sister.

"Gus got stuck at the farm, so he called me to pick up the kids. He said to say he was sorry. He really wanted to be here."

"I'll go gather the kids' things," Polly said, leaving the two women standing alone on the playground. Rusty was supervising the sandbox, where the boys were playing and Willow was pushing Lily and Dulcie on the swings. Christy Perez was playing on the seesaw with Emma Morgan, who had just arrived for afterschool care.

Lynn forced a smile as she turned to Laurie. "So, are you all packed up and ready to go?"

"Pretty much. Most of the furniture is already out at the new house. Gus has made arrangements for the rest to get moved next week."

Lynn nodded but stayed silent, watching Dulcie laughing, her cheeks rosy, eyes bright.

"She's doing so great, isn't she?" Laurie said, following her gaze.

"She's a sweetheart. We're gonna miss her and Cal."

"They'll be back before you know it."

"Maybe," Lynn said, instantly regretting it.

"This is his home now, Lynn. Their home. I saw it the minute I arrived this time."

"Yes, but look what he's going to."

"It's temporary, from what I understand. They're apparently grooming one of Mr. Morgan's kids to take over."

"Maybe."

"My brother is crazy about you. That's why *this* is home."

Lynn turned to her. "I'm not sure what he is or isn't, Laurie, but thanks for saying it."

Polly brought the children's backpacks, blankets, and artwork, and she helped Laurie load everything into the truck. Finally, they called the kids and gave each a hug and bags with cards from all the other children. As Laurie hugged Lynn, she whispered, "They'll be back, I promise. And my stupid brother will come to his senses soon."

"Safe trip," Lynn said, winking at Dulcie and ruffling Cal's hair. "Let us know when you're home safe now."

And then they were gone. Cal's sister and his beautiful children of whom she had grown so fond.

Three weeks later, Lynn, whose cycle, unlike Polly's, was very regular, was late. A week later, she began to feel nauseous. After a week of nausea, she visited the pharmacy. That evening, she administered the test and learned what she'd known for ten days. *The Valley baby boom has added another member to its ranks!*

CHAPTER 26

"I can't believe it! This is sooo exciting!" Polly said when Lynn shared her news.

"I'm glad you think so."

"What do you mean? Aren't you thrilled? We'll have our babies together."

"*If* I have a baby."

"Lynn, you can't mean you would?"

"Jesus, Poll, I don't know what I mean. Of course I want this baby, but what about all this?" She waved her hands. "Who's gonna run the Cottage?"

"We are. It's perfect."

"I'm not sure our employers will agree. You're a married woman, so it may be fine for you, but me?"

"The Morgans are some of the most broad-minded people I know. Talk to them, and talk to Gus. I'm sure you'll be a married woman before that baby arrives."

"Ever the optimist, aren't you? Here come the kids, Pollyanna," Lynn said as Maggie Morgan opened the door and Ben the third ran in, Emma on his heels.

"Morning, ladies!" In her usual jeans and ranch T-shirt, Maggie looked as gorgeous as ever, her long thick hair tied back in a ponytail.

"Morning," Polly said. "Hi, Ben, hi, Emma!"

"How are you making out?" Maggie asked as she stowed Ben's things. "A little less hectic now that you're down two?"

"It's been a fun summer so far. They love going over to camp to swim and see the horses."

"And we love having them. It's been the best year yet for Emma's Dream. We're even talking about expanding next summer to allow us to take more campers. The word's out now, and the waiting list is so long. We feel really badly saying no to so many kids."

"It's an incredible place you've created," Lynn said. "Only camp I've ever heard of that rivals Emma's Dream is Jabberwocky on Martha's Vineyard."

"Yes, I know Jabberwocky. They were super helpful when we were planning the camp."

"I worked there two summers when I was a teenager. Never knew the founder, Helen Lamb, but her vision sure lives on."

Maggie smiled, watching her rambunctious son out of the corner of her eye. "How's he been?"

"Fine. Full of beans as usual," Lynn said.

"That's good, 'cause with his dad away, he's been hell on wheels at home. Emma and I are at our wits' end."

"When's the pack trip get back?" Lynn asked, referring to the first of two pack trips run out of Morgan's Run each summer. Expensive and exclusive, they were a cash cow for the ranch. Trips usually counted celebrities among the riders, and this trip was no exception. Superstar singer Jess Corey and her entourage had booked the current trip.

"Three days, and we're counting the minutes, aren't we, Em?"

Emma smiled, then headed over to sit with her cousins Lily and Charlotte.

"She's my rock. Don't know what I'd do without her."

"What a trip," Lynn said. "I mean, Jess Corey. Wow. They'll probably have great campfire sing-alongs."

Maggie rolled her eyes. "I doubt that, although she has agreed to come and sing at camp the night after they get back."

"After a day of spa treatments?"

"I'm sure."

"Have you heard from them?"

"Ben reached us yesterday, and things have been pretty smooth. Just the usual theatrics and saddle sores. This is an easy trip. No mountain passes or steep ridgeline crossings after the last trip." The previous season, there had been an accident on the trail where a rider and horse had fallen. Both survived, but the woman ended up with a broken leg.

"That's good," Lynn said. "You nearly lost Kyle last year, right?"

Maggie smiled. "The Morgan brothers are tough. Sisters too, although Ruthie's about to go crazy without Harley. What was he thinking going on this trip with the farm and baby Charlotte?"

"He was thinking about the fun he'd have with his buddy Ben."

"Don't I know it! Oh, this afternoon, my dad'll pick up the kids. Ruthie's practically living at the Big House until Harley gets back, so Leonora and Ben have their hands full."

"Of course."

"Well, gotta run. I'd love to hang out here with you guys, though," Maggie said, her voice wistful.

Lynn smiled. "Any day."

"Before I go, how are *you* doing? I imagine you miss Gus."

Surprised, Lynn didn't know what to say. Finally, she shrugged.

"I'm sorry," Maggie said. "I didn't mean to pry."

"It's okay. Yes, I do miss him."

"Well, he'll be home before you know it."

"Maybe."

"There's no maybe about it. Ben and Spark signed paperwork yesterday. A mustang rescue center is officially coming to Valley Stables, and Gus is going to run it."

"What about Tom Jacobi or Harley?"

"It was Harley's idea, and Tom's too busy with the thoroughbreds. Gus is the man, you can count on it. He's got a way with horses, like our Nick. You can't teach that, it's just in a person. Have you ever seen him with a horse?"

Lynn shook her head, realizing she knew next to nothing about that aspect of Gus's life. *So much I don't know,* she thought sadly. "Won't Richard Morgan fight hard to keep him back east?"

"Not if he wants to maintain good relations with his brother." Maggie patted her arm. "He'll be back. Have a great day." With that, she hurried to kiss her children, then flew out the door.

CHAPTER 27

Gus looked out at the rolling fields and woods at the edge of the farm proper, temporarily called Morgan's Run East. Richard Morgan claimed the name was temporary only until they could come up with a better one. They were busy with hiring, and scouts were out searching for horses. Stella had arrived the day after Gus had, and she was settling in. He spent as much time as he could with her.

Jesus, I miss you, Lynn, he mused, every thought in his downtime about her and the kids. He spoke to Dulcie and Cal at least twice a day and had called Lynn several times. Their conversations had been subdued. The distance had shaken him, and he ached for her in his arms and the kids on his lap. He often read to them at night on FaceTime, but it wasn't the same. Every trip to Wyoming ended in tears.

After a month in Massachusetts with two trips home for weekends with the kids, he had settled into a routine, but progress was slow going. Richard Morgan, while a great guy, was not his brother or Spark. He took forever to make decisions, and there were also his kids, who were jockeying for positions in this brand-new venture. Richard Junior and his sister, Gail, both worked for their dad. Richard had gone to Wharton and ran the business end of things for the farm and a host of other Morgan Inc. businesses. He and Gail oversaw the day-to-day operations, but she was a people person, he was not. Weezie was in grad school for social work at Boston University, but had taken a break claiming she wanted to work with the horses and the mustang program. Her father had not yet agreed to this, but it was impossible to ignore her rapport with all animals.

The farm and its two hundred acres included a large farmhouse, two smaller cottages, several barns, and smaller outbuildings. Workers were toiling round the clock constructing a state-of-the-art stables, indoor riding center, and two racetracks. The main farmhouse had been gutted, and Richard Morgan Senior was living in a rented house nearby during the remodel, due to be completed by early September. After the farmhouse and stables projects, he intended to renovate or build cottages for employees of the farm. Unmarried, Richard Junior rented a small house in nearby Horseshoe Crab Cove and had expressed no interest in living on the property. Gail and Weezie lived with their dad. Wolfie, who worked part-time at the farm, lived an hour away in Boston, and the rest of the eight Morgan siblings lived elsewhere.

Gus rented a studio apartment from Lucy Winthrop Brennan, Helen's daughter, who lived in Somers, the next town to the north of Horseshoe Crab Cove. Her mother lived in the Cove. Gus's apartment was above the Brennans' garage and had a small kitchenette and bathroom. It was a beautiful property and had apparently been Lucy's ex-husband's family home. Her divorce agreement stipulated that once Amy, her youngest, left for college, she would give up the house. Rob, her ex, hadn't decided what to do with it. According to local gossip, he was still trying to win Lucy back. He rented a house in town and lived on and off with his girlfriend.

In the evenings, Lucy often invited Gus to the house for a drink or dinner, and she sometimes confided bits and pieces of her situation to him. Gus had met Rob Brennan several times, and, in his opinion, he wasn't half good enough for Lucy. Also, it was clear that his employer, Richard Morgan, had taken a shine to her and had been over to the house several times for dinner. Lucy usually included Gus at these dinners because her teenagers, Robert and Amy, loved his company and were clearly still ambivalent about their mother's suitor.

"Hey, Gus!" Weezie Morgan called, disturbing him from his reverie. "Penny for your thoughts." Dressed in skintight jeans and a T-shirt two sizes too small, she sashayed up and climbed the fence next to him.

He shrugged. "Not worth a penny. Just checking on the progress over here," he said, indicating the stables.

"If I had to guess, your thoughts were a bit farther west. Wanta come for a ride?"

"No, thanks."

"You know, a bunch of us are going up the coast tonight, to the Narrows. There's a great band playing. Wanta join us?"

He smiled. "Thanks, but I'll pass."

"Come on, you've gotta have fun sometimes. Must be so dull at the Brennans'."

"Actually, I'm enjoying myself."

"You'd enjoy yourself a lot more with me," she said, moving closer, her arm grazing his.

"Listen, Weezie, you're a terrific woman, but I'm your employee."

"My dad's employee. Just like me."

"The thing is—"

"I know, I know, you're in love with that day care lady, though heaven knows why."

He opened his mouth to defend Lynn, but then stayed silent, turning to go. "See ya," he called over his shoulder. "Have a good ride."

He thought he heard her mutter, "Bitch," but couldn't be certain. No matter, he was not the least bit interested in spoiled Weezie Morgan or her kind of fun.

On impulse, he pulled out his phone. It was seven in the morning in the Valley, and he hoped he might catch her. "Hey," she said, picking up after the first ring.

"Hey, yourself."

"How's it going?"

"Slow."

Lynn swallowed, knowing she should tell him about the baby, but couldn't. "Does that mean your time there will be extended?"

"Not too much, maybe through September, no longer."

"How are the kids?" she asked, sitting down on a stool in the Cottage kitchen. She was doing early setup this morning because Polly had a doctor's appointment.

"Good. They love being with my folks, but it's tough to leave them."

"You'll all be together soon."

"Yup. Lynn... I feel like we... You and I... Well, we left things sort of weirdly, and I'm sorry about that."

"Everything happened so quickly. Us, then the job, the move, everything." *Including my pregnancy!*

"Yeah, but I still feel like a shit. When are you coming east?"

"Two weeks."

"Any chance of us meeting?"

"I'm going to be at my parents' in Connecticut. It's probably about two hours from you. We could meet halfway, if you have free time? Maybe the weekend of the sixteenth?"

"Shit, I'll be in Wyoming. How about the next weekend?"

"I fly back that Saturday."

"I could probably take a day or two during the week. Text me your dates, and I'll work something out. I really want to see you."

"Me too," she said as Rusty stepped in and waved. "Gotta go. Take care of yourself."

"You too."

He slipped the phone into his pocket, smiling.

CHAPTER 28

Lynn regarded her friend at the end of a long Friday. "Hey, Poll, why don't you take off? Willow and I can handle this."

"I'm fine, just tired."

"I know, so go! You've been covering for me and the morning throw-ups."

"Dr. Blake says everything looks fine. My OB too."

"Dr. Blake and your OB are not here. I am, and you look like a ghost. Now go."

"I just wish we hadn't lent Rusty to the camp today."

"It's fine. We survived. When Willow finishes cleaning up outside, she and I can tidy up in here. Not much to do, and I can come in Sunday to button up before the cleaning brigade arrives." They were closing the Cottage for two weeks to allow Polly, Lynn, and the others to have a break. Leonora had professional cleaners coming Monday.

"But you have things to do."

"And three days to do 'em. I'm not leaving till Wednesday, whereas you're heading to Portland tomorrow, remember?"

"We could delay?" She, Kevin, and Jasper were traveling north to visit his family for a few days, then flying east for a week to see Polly's parents and siblings.

"Absolutely not. Gigi's called twice complaining about how your family gets you for longer than theirs."

"She's being ridiculous," Polly said. She loved Kevin's sister, but she was a pot stirrer. "We just saw the whole clan in June."

"Anyway, please take off, sweetie."

"Okay, but... Well... I'll miss you."

"Same here."

"Did you arrange to meet up with Gus?"

"Maybe. We'll see."

"I'm sure he'll move heaven and earth to make it happen."

Lynn laughed, hugging her partner. Polly was visibly pregnant now, but rail thin. "Okay, Pollyanna, take care of yourself and eat!"

"You too. And good luck with the Morgans. It's tonight, right?"

"Yup. Going over for a drink at six thirty."

"They'll be fine about it," Polly said.

"We'll see. Have a great trip." Lynn waved as Polly turned at the door and blew her a kiss. "Go!"

❧

Leonora Morgan greeted her at the front door. "We're delighted to see you, Lynn dear. Come out back to the terrace. Ben's having a beer, I'm having white wine. What can we get you?"

"Seltzer would be great, thanks."

Leonora gave her a look, then waved toward the terrace doors. "Head on out. I'll just pop in and get your drink."

"Well, this is a treat for us old fogies," Ben Morgan said, rising to hug Lynn. "We can celebrate your much-deserved vacation."

"Thanks, Ben," she said, taking a seat next to him. "Honestly, every day's a vacation here, but it will be good to see my family."

"Your other family, you mean," Leonora said, stepping onto the terrace and handing her a tall glass of seltzer with lime. "You know we consider you and Polly dear family members."

"Yes, and we're very blessed by your kindness and warmth."

"When do you fly east?" he asked.

"Wednesday."

"Do you have a ride to the airport?"

"I'm going to leave my car, thanks."

"Well, let us know, if you'd like a ride," he said. "We're always looking for something to do."

"I hardly think so with all your activities. I hear things are buzzing at the farm, and the Cowbelles must be in full swing with the Fair."

Leonora waved her hand. "Oh pish, tush. That fair almost runs itself after all these years. The camp's another story. Poor Carm has been back and forth assisting since their cook, Johnny, took sick. He's better now, thank goodness."

"If I wasn't going home, I'd be happy to volunteer over there. When I get back, I'll have a few days. I can check in with Maggie."

"Nonsense!" Leonora said. "You take every second of your vacation time, sweetie. Now, much as we love to have you visit, we know you have something on your mind."

"Yes," Lynn said quietly. "And I don't want to delay your dinner."

"No worries about that," Ben said. "In fact, we'd love for you to join us."

"Oh, thank you, but I'm meeting a friend in town. So...it's a personal matter," she said.

"We figured as much," he said.

"I'm... Well, I'm pregnant."

Leonora's face registered surprise, then she threw up her hands. "Thank goodness! I mean, congratulations! We were so afraid you were going to tell us you're quitting."

Ben smiled, reaching over to pat Lynn's hand. "Happy for you, darlin'. We've got a mini baby boom goin' on around here, don't we?"

"Beth's pregnant too," Leonora whispered. "But please don't say a word."

"And our Rosie and Polly. We built the Cottage just in time."

"That's what I wanted to speak with you about," she said, realizing that neither Morgan had asked about the father. "The Cottage. Polly and I will both have babies, who I'm assuming can come with us to work, but I wasn't sure how you felt about that. With all the babies coming, another staff member might be needed. Also, both of your directors would, in some ways, be compromised. That's not the right word, but you know what I mean? Maybe distracted a little?"

"Not a bit of it!" he said.

"I would understand if you wanted me to step down or search for a new director," Lynn said.

"Is that what *you* want, honey?" Leonora asked.

"No, I love my job, but this is your venture, and we're caring for your grandchildren."

"And we wouldn't want those precious babies with anyone else," Ben said.

Leonora nodded, agreeing with her husband. "Honey, this is why we built the Cottage. To care for all our beloved children. Your and Polly's children will be cherished like our own babies. And, we have complete confidence in your ability to handle both roles of mommy and teacher."

"We sure do. Any extra staff you need, just say the word, and we and Spark will get right on it."

Lynn's eyes filled with tears. "Thank you. Thank you both so much."

"No, darlin', it's we who should be thanking you," he said.

"That's right," Leonora said, regarding her with kind eyes. "I don't mean to pry, but is this a happy turn of events for you, honey?"

Wiping tears away, Lynn said, "Yes, despite these, I'm happy about the baby. It took some adjustment because it was unexpected, but yes, I'm happy."

Leonora set down her empty wineglass. "Good! That's all we needed to know."

Lynn swallowed. They hadn't asked, but she needed to tell them. "Gus Casey is the father."

"I'm sure he's as thrilled as we are," Ben said.

"He doesn't know," she said, "I'm hoping to see him for a day when I'm back east. I'll tell him then."

"We won't breathe a word," Leonora said.

"Thank you," Lynn said, drinking the last of her seltzer. "Now, I'll let you get to your dinner."

They walked her to her car, wishing her a safe trip. "And after Nora's cleaning army is finished, the Cottage'll be all spick and span for you and the kids when you return," Ben said.

Lynn smiled at her hosts, who stood arm in arm. The most loving couple she knew. *To find love like that,* she mused, hugging them and hopping into her car.

"Safe travels, honey!" Leonora called as she drove out.

CHAPTER 29

"Welcome to weirdo land," Barb Manguilli said to her sister as Lynn unpacked.

"What's new with Mom and Dad?"

"Same ole same ole. At least we're not in the middle of it anymore."

Their parents were divorced, but still shared the same waterfront property in Groton, Connecticut. Their mom lived in the large rambling shingled house and their father in the two-bedroom carriage house at the opposite end of the estate.

"We're all going to dinner tomorrow night, I hear."

"Yup. More weirdness."

"Are Barry and Molly coming?"

"Yup."

"The kids?"

"To Chez Maarten with Dad? I don't think so. No, they weren't invited."

"Geez."

"They'll be over Sunday for the day."

"Good," Lynn said. She loved her niece and nephew and hated being so far away from them.

"So, what's new? You look great, by the way."

"Thanks."

"Kind of glowing," Barb said, studying her. "Who's the guy?"

"It's not that, believe me," Lynn said, plopping down on the bed beside her. "I mean there is a guy. His name is Gus. He's amazing, but we're kind of in a limbo state right now." She related highlights of the relationship up until the present and his job back east.

"So are you gonna see him while you're here? Or, more importantly, am *I* gonna meet him?"

"Maybe, we're trying to figure something out."

"Is he good-looking?"

"Yes."

"So if Mr. Hot and Handsome isn't the reason why you're glowing, what is?"

Lynn looked over at her. "I'm pregnant."

"No!"

"And I haven't told Mom or Dad. I'm not sure I will, at least not for a few months."

"She's gonna know something's up the minute she sees you, sis. You know how she is. ESP doesn't begin to describe Sorcha Super Sleuth. Plus, you should see yourself. You've changed."

Lynn shrugged. "Well, if she drags it out of me, so be it, but I'd rather not have the whole visit be about her wringing her hands and trying to find solutions for my big problem." Sorcha Manguilli was a child psychiatrist, as was her ex-husband, Sol. They had met in medical school and still consulted each other on cases from time to time.

"She's gonna know the minute you pass on wine for dinner. I mean, it's Chez Maarten. Dad'll be buying three-hundred-dollar bottles of who knows what."

Lynn laughed. "So are you saying no one's ever eaten a meal at Chez Maarten without swilling down gallons of overpriced wine?"

"Not in this family. I'd prepare yourself for the Inquisition."

∾

Sunday afternoon found Lynn and her family in Adirondack chairs facing the river, watching Barry and Molly's kids roll around with Sorcha's precious French bulldogs. Their Friday night dinner had gone smoothly, although it was clear her mother's radar was up. Lynn had been avoiding her all weekend, shopping with Barb, seeing friends, and taking long walks. Gus had phoned on his way to the airport Sunday morning to say that he could break free for the day and night Wednesday, so she'd made reservations at a B and B in Newport, Rhode Island, as well as dinner reservations at the Fluke, her favorite Newport restaurant. She smiled, closing her eyes, basking in the sun. *Lovely to have Wednesday night to look forward to with all its possibilities.*

"Okay, Lynnie," her mother said, interrupting her reverie. "Everyone's out of earshot and it's just you and me. What's going on?"

Startled, she opened her eyes to spy Barry, Molly, Barb, and her father all chasing the kids down by the water's edge. "I'm enjoying this weather and time with my family." She squinted up at her stylish parent, who looked more like her sister than her mom. Sorcha's salt-and-pepper hair was cut in a short, stylish bob, held back by designer sunglasses that probably cost a month of Lynn's salary. She was dressed in capris and a simple linen top, flip-flops on her pedicured feet.

"Lynn Manguilli, don't play coy with me. You aren't drinking, you are floating on cloud nine one moment, in the dumps the next. I'm assuming there's a man in this picture, but I'm also assuming you're pregnant."

Lynn looked out on the river, sighed, and turned to face her, shielding her eyes against the sun. "Yes, Mother, I'm pregnant. Yes, there's a man. He doesn't know about the baby. I just found out myself."

"And?"

"And what?"

"What are you going to do about it?"

"The baby?"

"The whole mess!"

"There's no mess."

"How are you going to support yourself?"

"I have a job, remember? It pays me a huge salary and has wonderful benefits."

"But what about when the baby comes?"

"He or she will come with me."

"That's absurd. What will your employers think of that?"

"They're thrilled and very supportive."

"I don't believe you."

Lynn sat up, now at the edge of her seat. "Mom, I've got this. I want the baby. I'm having the baby. Period, end of story."

"What about the father?"

"I'm seeing him this Wednesday."

"Oh, is he coming east?"

"He's working in Massachusetts temporarily."

"Oh, now I see why we're graced with your presence. You really came east to see him."

"Mom, Gus had nothing to do with me coming home. This trip was planned way before I knew he'd be back here or that I'd be pregnant. I just think he should know about the baby, and I want to tell him in person. I extended my time here by two days to make up for the quick overnight to Newport."

"Oh, so you're having an overnight with this Gus person. Gus? What kind of a name is that anyway? Is it short for Augustus?"

"I have no idea."

"You mean to tell me that you're having this man's baby and you don't even know his full name?"

Lynn stood. "This is why I didn't say anything earlier." She stalked off to join the others on the beach.

"Lynn! I'm not finished talking!"

Well, I am.

CHAPTER 30

Richard Morgan caught him early Wednesday morning. "Hey, Gus, you leaving soon?"

"Not till noon. We've got a pretty full morning."

"You're doing terrific work. Just wish everything moved a little faster."

"Any word on that?"

"Equipment's on the way. The stables won't be completed till mid-September. I've got a firm commitment from the contractors with cash attached. They're working straight through Labor Day."

Poor guys, Gus thought. He liked Richard Morgan, but sometimes people like him didn't get the life of blue-collar workers. *Even if he does pay them overtime, they're still giving up a long weekend with their families. Not unlike me.* Money had bought his extended time away from his family. "Mustangs are settling in," he said, indicating the nearby corral, where five of the wild horses grazed.

"Glad to hear it. Listen, Gus, I have a huge favor to ask. Something for you to think about on your getaway. You know I'd like to keep you full-time, but I've given up the ghost on that one. What I'm asking is for you to stay through September. It's just two more weeks. I don't have to tell you what a critical time it is for us."

"I'm pretty sure that between them, Dennis, Rich, Weezie, and Gail can handle things. They've already hired some good people."

"But not a trainer. Not someone who understands horses like you do."

"You know I can't stay on indefinitely?"

"I know, buddy, I know. But two weeks would really help. Obviously, I'll double your salary, and if you'd like, I can send the jet to fly your family out for a long weekend."

"Let me think about it and talk to my folks. I'll let you know in a day or two."

The older man patted him on the shoulder. "Thanks, buddy. I appreciate it. By the way, Lucy Brennan's coming by in an hour. Have we got two horses that are gentle enough for her and this old tenderfoot?"

Gus had seen Richard in the saddle. He had grown up riding, so while he might be a bit rusty, he could handle most horses. "Crackers and Sheba are probably the gentlest. I'd recommend you ride Crackers. Want me to have one of the guys saddle 'em up for you?"

"Let's wait and see if she shows up. It was kind of a 'come over if you're free' kind of thing."

Whatever that means, Gus thought. "Okay, just let us know. I'll be out with the mustangs."

AFTER HELPING LUCY UP ON SHEBA, THE GENTLE CHESTNUT MORGAN, Gus turned to his employer, who hopped onto Crackers, an American Paint, without assistance. Their mounts were stable horses, purchased to use for lessons and as companions for the thoroughbreds. The companions idea was Gus's as he believed thoroughbreds performed better when they were well socialized. "All set?" he asked.

"Thanks, Gus. We're planning to head down and take the Loop Trail around Horseshoe Crab Cove."

"That's a long ride. You sure you're up to it?" Gus shaded his eyes, watching Sheba pace, Lucy's hold on the reins tentative. "The Loop itself is about eighteen miles, and you've got a mile or two from here before you hook up with it."

"What do you think?" Richard asked his companion.

"I'm happy to give it a try," she said, sounding not at all enthusiastic.

Gus smiled, patting Sheba's flank. "Well, you can give it a go. If you get to the Loop and want to turn back, that's an option. And," he added, "may I?" She handed him the reins. "If you hold her a little more firmly, she'll feel calmer. Like this."

"Thanks," she said softly.

Gus didn't know Helen Winthrop's daughter well, but he liked her. Not only was she lovely, but he glimpsed traces of sadness flickering in her blue eyes. He smiled up at her. "You'll do fine. Have a great ride." He then turned to his boss. "I'm taking off soon. Dennis'll be waiting when you get back. He'll take care of the horses."

"Thanks, Gus. Have a good trip, and please think about my offer."

Gus waved. "Will do."

That was all he thought about on the drive to Newport. *Two more weeks away from my babies and Lynn.*

CHAPTER 31

"Of course you can meet him, as long as you don't stay all day and night," Lynn said to her sister. They sat on a bench at Bowen's Wharf sharing an enormous burger filled with cheese, mushrooms, and bacon. Lynn's hands were outstretched so the delicious sauce fell on the cobblestones, not her lap.

"I'll be gone in a flash, don't you worry. I've gotta get to Boston anyway. This burger is sinful. Thank God we didn't each get one." Barb wiped sauce from her mouth. "You've got a great day for it."

"It?"

"You know, exploring with your honey. What are you gonna do anyway?"

"I haven't a clue. We'll decide together."

"When's he coming?"

"Any minute, as I told you five minutes ago."

"Think he'll notice?"

"I'm not showing."

"No, but you forget about the glow." Barb leaned back, studying her. "It's not too noticeable today, or maybe I've just gotten used to the new you."

"Ha-ha."

"Seriously, sis, I'm happy for you. Really, I am."

"Thanks, but let's not count the chickens yet."

"God, look at the size of that yacht!"

Barb pointed at a huge sailboat motoring by, but Lynn wasn't looking at the water. She'd spotted Gus walking toward them, his eyes scanning the crowds. Six weeks! She had missed him with every fiber of her being. All she wanted was to jump into his arms and smother him with kisses, but she took a deep breath, stuffed her wrapper into the takeout bag, and poked her sister. "Lose this trash. He's coming."

Barb stood with her, watching as Lynn waved and Gus spied her. His look was unmistakable. *He's in love with my sister, big-time!*

WHEN LYNN REACHED HIM, GUS OPENED HIS ARMS AND SHE FELL INTO them. "Oh boy, am I glad to see you," he said, holding her, kissing her.

"Me too," she said, her heart nearly bursting. Suddenly, she remembered Barb. "My sister's here. She wants to meet you, okay?"

"Of course," he said, looking around until he spied the petite, dark-haired woman several yards away, waving and grinning. He could see the family resemblance, the young woman's sparkling eyes and smile so like her sister's.

"Hey, hi," she said, stepping forward to join them. "I'm Barb."

"Great to meet you," he said, extending his hand, which Barb ignored as she hugged him.

Lynn watched, amused by her sister's behavior and Gus's reaction. "Where are you parked?" she asked.

"A couple of streets up. This is a hopping place, isn't it?"

"This is Newport in the summer," Barb said. "So we're parked that way. Why don't we head back and grab Lynn's things, and I can give you the third degree while we walk." She latched on to Gus's arm and propelled him forward, winking over her shoulder at Lynn.

They said goodbye at Barb's Mini Cooper. More hugs. "So good to meet you, Gus. I hope you guys have an awesome time. Sis, you gonna be okay to get back tomorrow?"

"All set," Lynn said, "See you in a couple of days?"

"Not sure. I'll either stay one or two nights in Boston. I'll text you." With that, she called, "Toodle-loo!" and drove off, leaving them on the sidewalk.

Feeling suddenly shy, she said, "What do you think? Should we explore? Check in to the B and B?"

"Is the B and B far?"

"A couple of blocks."

"Then I vote for checking in, getting our bearings, then making a plan."

"You have my vote," she said, kissing him lightly. "So good to see you."

Gus squeezed her hand. "Come on, my car's not far."

CHAPTER 32

"Hey, folks, welcome." A round-faced blonde with rosy apple cheeks swung open the door soon after they rang the bell. "You must be the Manguillis. Come on in. I'm Dottie Periwinkle, owner and proprietor here."

Gus said, "Hello. Great house."

"Thank you, dear."

Lynn smiled as they stepped into the hallway sandwiched between two parlors filled with what appeared to be relatively comfortable Victorian furnishings. "I wondered where the B and B's name originated, and now I know."

Dottie winked. "It's named for my favorite sea creature, periwinkles. I had my name legally changed when I bought it after my divorce. Got rid of my ex's hideous name in the bargain. Come, sit, or are you eager to get to your room and freshen up?"

"Having some time to freshen up sounds great," Lynn said quickly.

"Good choice! We can always catch up over a glass of sherry later. Or not. My guests should not feel obligated to spend one minute with me." She went to a large antique desk at the far end of the hall, opened the top with a key, and extracted an oversized periwinkle-blue envelope, which she handed to Lynn. "There you are, dear."

The envelope read "The Manguillis," and Gus murmured, "Gus Manguilli, hmm."

Lynn turned to Dottie, "I'm Lynn Manguilli, and this is Gus Casey."

"Well, I am very pleased to make your acquaintance. Your room is the last door on the left upstairs. I only have one other guest tonight, so it should be nice and quiet for you. My rooms are in the annex behind the kitchen, and my cell number is on the information in your welcome packet. Call anytime. Sherry, tea, biscuits, and other treats are always in the blue parlor. Breakfast is in the green parlor. Anytime between seven and ten. You let me know what works for you. I can also make a tray for your room."

Dottie brushed her hands together. "I think that's it. I have plenty of snacks in the kitchen too. Please help yourself. Pantry on the left, just inside the door."

"Thanks, Dottie," Gus said, his hand on the small of Lynn's back, guiding her toward the stairs. "I'm sure we'll be very comfortable."

"Enjoy your stay." Dottie winked. "I'm guessing I won't be seeing much of you two."

He took both bags and followed Lynn up the narrow staircase. Anticipating what lay ahead, Lynn could barely walk. Her knees wobbled, and her body was on fire.

"Oh my God, I've died and gone to heaven," Gus said, tossing the bags aside and closing the door of their room.

"It's lovely, isn't it?" she said, gazing around the very large suite with a queen four-poster covered with an off-white embroidered quilt. There was a sitting area, where she predicted they would spend no time, and a beautiful bath with a huge claw-foot tub.

"Not as lovely as you. Come here," he said, drawing her into his arms. "I've missed you so much, my sweet girl."

In answer, Lynn kissed him, her tongue twined round his, hungry for him. His hands were everywhere, gently raising her T-shirt over her head before dropping it to the floor. As she arched her neck, his lips moved down to between her breasts, trailing soft, whisper kisses that threatened to send her over the edge. She reached round and unclasped her bra, offering herself to him.

"Oh, baby," he said, voice husky as he fondled and teased her nipples.

Lynn unbuttoned his shirt, her hands caressing as they moved down to his belt. His arousal was hard against her belly, and she swiftly unzipped his jeans, releasing him, embracing him, her hands moving up and down, stroking the way she'd already discovered he liked. She knew he didn't need a condom, but didn't want to shatter the moment with her news. She said nothing as he slipped one on and eased them onto the bed.

His fingers slid between her legs, and Gus smiled. "That's my girl. You're ready for me."

She nodded, and in one deft move, he parted her legs and plunged into her, partway at first, then deeper and deeper as she caressed and encouraged him with every part of her body.

"Oh Gus, I... I..." she murmured, arching up to meet his every thrust until it felt as if she might split in two with raw primal feeling. "More, more, more!" she cried as they came to a spectacular climax, bodies in perfect synch.

As they lay entwined in the aftermath, he kissed her softly. "I wonder if Dottie heard that down in her kitchen."

"I'm sure she's heard plenty over the years, and I don't care," Lynn said, snuggling against him. "At this moment, I'm blissfully sated and happy."

"Oh, Lynn, it's so good to see you."

She nestled against his shoulder, warm for the first time since he departed. "Mmm."

They slept for a short time, made languorous love again, then decided to do a little exploring. As they dressed, she told him about the dinner reservations, and he said, "Fine with me as long as it's not too dressy. I only have these kinds of clothes."

"You're perfect. It's a seafood place, casual, but great food."

"Only thing I ask is that you and me take a swim in that tub at some time during this visit."

"You read my mind," she said, kissing him, then grabbing her bag.

CHAPTER 33

A perfect summer day for walking the historic city, there was a breeze blowing from the ocean that tempered the heat of the August sun. Since Gus had never been to Newport, she suggested they tour one mansion, then hike the Cliff Walk, a path above the cliffs with spectacular ocean views on one side and close-up peeks at the "summer cottages" lining the walkway. These elegant mansions with their beautiful gardens and sweeping lawns had been the summer homes of the wealthy in the city's golden age. Some were still privately owned, while many had become holdings of the Newport Preservation Society and were open to the public.

After a tour of the Breakers, the most famous of the summer cottages, originally built and owned by Cornelius Vanderbilt, they walked along Bellevue Avenue to Memorial Boulevard then onto the start of the Cliff Walk. They held hands, talking amiably about Valley life and Richard Morgan's new stables. While comforted by his nearness and presence, Lynn's mind was unsettled as she anticipated telling him about the pregnancy. *What will he say? Will it destroy our precious time together?*

They reached a rocky beach area at the far end of the walk, and she swallowed hard. "Gus, that path leads back to Bellevue It's only a short walk from this end to the B and B. Can we sit a minute?"

"Of course," he said, eying her. "You look pale. Are you okay?"

She sat on a flat boulder and patted the space beside her. "I'm fine. There's...there's something I have to tell you."

"Of course." He sat and took her hands in his, green eyes soft.

"I wanted to tell you earlier, but wanted... Well, it's the kind of thing you want to say in person."

"I love you too," he said.

Lynn smiled at his kind face, so open and caring. "I love you, but that's not it. I... We... I'm... Well, I'm pregnant. I don't know how or when it happened, but the baby is yours. I don't know how you feel about it, and I'm not asking for anything." As she spoke, his expression changed from warmth to shock. "I have already made the decision to keep the baby. If it's too much for you with Dulcie and Cal, I understand. I just thought you should know.

"Gus? Gus, are you okay?"

"When?"

"I don't know. I'm guessing one of those times we thought a condom might do double duty?"

He smiled. "No, I mean when is the baby due?"

"Oh, March, sometime in March."

"Are you okay? I mean are you feeling okay?"

"A little morning sickness, but otherwise fine. I talked to the Morgans before I came east, and they were very supportive about both their day care directors being with child, then parenting and running the Cottage."

"I'm not surprised," he said quietly.

A chill ran through her. Lynn tried to discern Gus's reaction. He seemed almost numb, distant. Abruptly, she stood. "I think we should head back."

"Okay," he said, following her up the path.

They walked in uncomfortable silence on the rough dirt path that led back to the streets of Newport. As they regained the sidewalk and started along Bellevue Lynn felt unbidden tears welling up. *He's gone. I don't know what I expected, but it appears I'll be raising this baby alone.*

Lynn nodded to Dottie as they entered the B and B. Sherry in hand, she was holding court in the blue parlor, a young couple sitting beside her. "Join us, dears!" she called, but Lynn was already halfway up the stairs. "Thanks," Gus said. "We've gotta get ready for dinner."

When he reached the room, Lynn had taken her bag into the bathroom and shut the door. He changed shirts and grabbed a sweater, then sat on the sofa, gazing out at Dottie's garden, a riotous mix of colors, slightly wild and overgrown. Finally, Lynn emerged. She had changed into a pale green summer dress and thin, strappy sandals, her hair pulled back, wearing silver earrings and necklace. She almost glowed in the fading light.

"You look beautiful," he said softly.

"Thanks. I'm ready if you are." She grabbed her bag and made for the door.

Gus wanted to speak, to say something that would make things right, to smooth things over so they could regain what they'd had only hours before, but instead, he stayed silent.

CHAPTER 34

After the waiter took their order, Gus reached across and took her hand. "I want to explain, Lynn. I'm happy for you if you want the baby. It's just a weird situation."

She took a sip of her seltzer, then met his eyes. "Weird how?"

"I made a promise, you see. To Lissie. It was just after Cal was born. They said she had to go to the operating room immediately. I wasn't allowed to come. She was bleeding heavily and in a lot of pain. I think she knew she wasn't going to make it. She kissed her dad, who was with us, then as I walked the gurney down the hall, she grabbed my arm and made me promise to find a nice woman, but never to marry or have any more children. I brushed her off saying, 'Don't worry, everything's going to be fine,' but she wouldn't let go so they could take her. Finally, the doctor said, 'Mr. Casey, if you want to save your wife, give her what she wants, now!' So I did. I promised. And those were the last words we exchanged. She bled out shortly after. There was nothing they could do." Tears rimmed his eyes, and he wiped them with his napkin.

Stunned, Lynn stared at him as if he were a stranger. She didn't know what to say. They were still sitting in silence when the waiter brought their meals. Neither ate much, and they declined dessert and coffee. As Gus paid the bill, Lynn thought, *How sad that I will have this memory of my favorite restaurant.*

They returned to the B and B, washed and slipped into bed, saying little. When she flicked out the light, he asked, "Can I hold you?" and Lynn slid over into his arms. He kissed her forehead, and she fell asleep heartbroken.

She rose early and showered and changed. When she stepped out of the bathroom, he was dressed, bag packed, sitting on the edge of the bed. "Shall we have breakfast before we head back?" she asked, still not sure how she was going to get back to Connecticut. She had assumed Gus might drive her, but *now*, she thought, *train or bus might be best.* Numb with shock and sadness, she followed him downstairs. He insisted on paying. While he was settling up with Dottie, she aimlessly poured herself a cup of tea from the sideboard.

A few minutes later, Dottie brought them a full breakfast of grapefruit, eggs, bacon, sausage, hash browns, toast, and a basket of wonderful-smelling muffins. "She's going to be really hurt if we don't eat this," Lynn whispered across the table.

Gus smiled. "Agreed," and dug into his very full plate.

As they finished breakfast, she said, "Would you mind dropping me at the bus station?"

"I can take you back, Lynn. Please, it's the least I can do."

"It's way out of your way."

"No, it isn't. I'm not expected back till late afternoon, so we have plenty of time."

"I'd like to get back this morning, if possible," she said, her voice ragged. "No point hanging around Newport."

"Okay, then I'll drive you. That's settled."

The silence on the drive was deafening. As they neared the Groton exit, he said, "How much longer are you staying with your folks?"

"Only a few days."

"There was so much I wanted to hear about them."

"Not much to tell. Mom and Dad'll be at work this morning. They're both psychiatrists. Not sure if I told you that before? They'll have a field day shrinking me after this. It's this street," she said, pointing. "Second driveway on the water side."

Gus pulled in and stopped in front of the house. "Lynn, I'm so sorry. I don't know what to say. I just need time to think things over."

"I understand," she said, quietly. "What you haven't said spoke volumes, though. I won't ask you in, 'cause I think you and I are visited out. Do you know the way back from here?"

"GPS."

"Well then, thanks for the ride." She slid out of the car and grabbed her bag.

"Lynn, wait!"

"No, Gus, no," she said as she turned and walked away.

CHAPTER 35

"**D**eathbed promises are always tricky," Sorcha Manguilli said as mother and daughter sat drinking tea on the terrace. "So unfair to the living too."

"Mother, I really don't want to talk about this now, and certainly not when Dad's around. The last thing I need is both of you shrinking me."

"You know how we hate that expression, Lynnie. And we're your parents. We care about you. You've had a terrible shock from someone you trusted and loved. "

She's right, of course. Sorcha Manguilli is seldom wrong. It didn't make things any better. Her mother had arrived home after work to find Lynn a sobbing mess and had spent the last hour attempting to pick up the pieces. "Thanks, Mom. I'm grateful. I just don't want to dissect the psychology behind this right now, okay?"

"Of course, sweetie. Shall I ask Dad to come for dinner? Would that cheer you up? The bimbo's probably there, but if his presence will do you good, I'll grin and bear it."

Lynn laughed in spite of herself. "Thanks, but I can survive without Dad and Shelly tonight. He and I are having lunch at the Clam Shack tomorrow anyway."

"Then why don't you and I go out tonight? There's that great new Japanese restaurant in Mystic."

Lynn was about to say no, but changed her mind. "Sure, Mom, that'd be great."

They were just getting ready to leave when Barb pulled in. "Hey, ladies, where you off to?"

"The new Japanese place in Mystic," Sorcha said, "Wanta come?"

"I'm in!" Barb said, leaving her things in the car and hopping into the backseat of her mother's Mercedes SUV. "So, how was your night with Mr. Dishy?" she asked, patting Lynn's shoulders.

Before Lynn could answer, their mother said, "Mr. Dishy has broken your sister's heart."

"What?" Barb exclaimed.

"It's a long story," Lynn said wearily. She now regretted the decision to go out to dinner, but here they were. "I'll fill you in at the restaurant."

They ordered, and when the waiter disappeared, Lynn gave her sister a brief summary of the past twenty-four hours, at the conclusion of which Barb said, "That sucks, big-time."

"I told her that deathbed promises can be tricky," Sorcha said, holding up her hand as Lynn started to protest. "I'm only saying it again because we didn't finish talking about it. There's a lot of literature about this that suggests that these promises are not always written in stone or kept. The survivors often work through their feelings and decide to live their lives in the present without restraint. It does take time, though...to come to grips. To let go."

Lynn shook her head. "That's not gonna happen. So there's no point talking about it. I'm going to raise this baby on my own. He or she will have lots of love."

"Won't it be awkward being out there with him around?" Barb said. "I mean, you'll have to see him every day."

"Perhaps, but the Morgans have been so terrific and supportive that I want to give it a go. If it's too awful, I'll make other choices. For now, it will be fun for Polly and me to have our babies together."

"How's she doing anyway?" Sorcha asked. "Are they still monitoring her closely?"

"Yes, and they think everything's going fine. She's pretty determined."

"Brave girl," her mother said.

"Yes, and I'm going to be there with her every step of the way. We're each other's birthing coaches."

"What about her hubby?" Barb asked.

"Kevin'll be there too."

"I could come out when you deliver?" Barb said. "If you want me?"

"I'd love it," Lynn said, squeezing her hand.

"He doesn't deserve you, baby," Sol Manguilli said as they ate lobster rolls on the deck of the Clam Shack.

"Maybe not, but he's a good person, just confused. I mean, it's over between us, but I bear him no ill will."

"Well, I do!"

Lynn smiled at her handsome father. Erudite, scatterbrained, curious, and charming, he was lovable, even though he'd broken their mother's heart and theirs with his numerous affairs. Shelly was just the latest in a long line of paramours. Lynn and Barb gave up meeting and getting to know Sol's girlfriends. No sense getting attached to someone who'd be gone in six months. "Thanks, oh champion of mine," she said. "All will be well. I have good friends in the Valley, and I know you guys are here if I want to come home."

"Of course we are. Want another tea?" he asked, waving his iced tea glass at the waiter.

"Sure, why not?"

Gus pulled into the farm at around two, finding his assistant, Dennis, and Weezie working with the mustangs. While his instinct was to retreat to his temporary office and talk to no one, he figured the distraction of work might help. He had always sought and found solace in the company of horses, and today was no exception. He stepped into the corral and spoke quietly to Demon, the tall black stallion no one dared touch but him. The horse reared up, snorted, then walked slowly toward him. Gus stood still, letting the animal come to him.

Weezie watched him, wondering at the behavior of man and horse. Gus looked like he'd just lost his best friend, and the mustang, who until a few minutes ago had been stirring up all his corral mates with his kicking, snorting, and nipping, was as docile as a lamb as he nudged Gus's shoulder, almost knocking him over. Slowly, Gus turned and gently rubbed his withers. Demon wasn't ready to have anyone touch his muzzle or the side of his head, but he allowed Gus's petting, standing tall, softly nickering.

"Welcome back," Weezie said. "You sure have the magic touch."

"Hey, boss," Dennis said.

"Hey," Gus said, closing his eyes, head resting against the huge mustang's rough, shaggy back.

CHAPTER 36

Gus threw himself into work for the rest of the day. When Weezie found him late in the afternoon, he was sitting on a bench, staring out at the corrals. "Hey, Gus, how was your trip? You didn't say before when Dennis asked."

"Fine, thanks."

"You don't look fine." Silence. "What'd you tell my dad? Are you gonna stay on longer?"

"Not sure. Told him I'd give him an answer tomorrow."

"So?"

"So, it's not tomorrow. Listen, Weezie, I gotta get going."

"I was going to ask you to have dinner with me."

"Thanks, maybe another night." He stood and tipped his hat, giving her a wan smile.

"I'm a good listener!" she called after his back.

Gus waved over his shoulder. He felt like all the life had been knocked out of him. He was scheduled to fly back to Wyoming the next day, but decided to postpone and take three or four days over Labor Day weekend. He loved Dulcie and Cal more than life itself, but without Lynn, the prospect of parenting suddenly felt overwhelming again, like it had in the days, weeks, and months after Lissie's death. *You'll get through it, buddy. You have to,* he told himself as he drove the short distance to Lucy Brennan's place. *A promise is a promise, no matter how hard it is now.*

LYNN ATTRIBUTED THE TEARS SAYING GOODBYE TO HER FAMILY TO hormones, although in truth it had been sad to leave them. Much as she hated to admit it, her parents' hovering had been comforting and some of their wisdom and advice helpful. She also hated to leave Barb, even though her sister would be headed back to school soon. Lynn smiled as she drove from the airport to her condo, thinking of Barb's parting words. "March, baby," she'd said, rubbing Lynn's tummy. "I'll take a leave from school if I have to, but I'm gonna be at this birth."

Polly had texted earlier, inviting her to dinner, and she'd accepted. Now, exhausted from the flight, she was a little sorry she'd said yes. Still, it would be good to be with friends.

"HEY, SWEETIE!" POLLY CRIED, OPENING THE DOOR A FEW HOURS LATER. "Kev and Jasper are at the Morgans catching up since Bennie and Jaspie seriously missed each other."

"Oh, Poll, you should have told me. You'd probably like to have gone too."

"No way, it's a guys' night. Maggie's got something going on at the camp, so she and Emma are down there. So it's the dads and little guys, and I have you all to myself. Come in, come in, I want to hear all about your trip, and I'll fill you in on mine."

Lynn hugged her friend, who was rail thin except for her baby bump. "How are you doing? Feeling okay?"

"Truth be told, the trip took a lot out of me," Polly said, pouring them both lemonades. "Let's sit outside. It's so beautiful tonight."

"And every night in the Valley," Lynn said, following her, tray of cheese, crackers, and olives in hand.

Once they settled, Lynn turned to her. "So did Gigi run you ragged in Portland?" She referred to Kevin's energetic younger sister.

Polly laughed. "Just a bit, and she's threatening to move to Arizona. She's been looking online at openings for nurses in this area. She's found a bunch in Tucson. She's also insisting she wants to be here for the birth. We'll probably have her and my mom jockeying for position in the delivery room."

"So I'm out?"

"Absolutely not! I've told them both that you and Kev are my coaches. Their jobs will be caring for Jasper. Oh, that's another person threatening to come out, Ivy, his aunt!" Ivy Robinson, who lived in Florida, was the sister of Jasper's deceased birth mother, Judith.

"Oh geez," Lynn said. "I hope Kevin is running interference for you."

"He's trying, but you know the cast of characters we're dealing with."

"How was your visit back east? I'm sorry we didn't hook up."

"After the whirlwind in Portland, I actually spent three of the five days in bed. My siblings entertained Kev and Jasper, which was great, and my mom waited on me hand and foot. As much as I hate her hovering, it was just what I needed."

Lynn smiled. "Sometimes we all need a little hovering."

"You too?" Polly asked, eyeing her. "You okay?"

"Body fine, heart maybe not. Gus and I kind of broke up."

"What! You saw him?"

"Yup. We planned a romantic night in Newport that got derailed by my news."

"I don't believe it! What happened?"

Lynn filled her in, ending with "Polly, I'm telling you all this 'cause you're my dear friend. And it's okay if you want to tell Kevin, but it's Gus's story to tell, so please don't mention it to anyone else."

"Of course not, but what will you say if people ask about you two?"

"We're friends, but that's all going forward. It's clear I'll be raising this baby on my own."

"Well, that's never gonna happen," Polly said, patting her hand. "You've got all of us and your family. Between all of us, your sweet baby will have lots of love. I'm just so surprised at Gus."

Lynn shrugged. "He made a promise. He's the kind of person who doesn't break promises."

"What about his promises to you? You don't just hop into a relationship like you guys have with something like that looming in the background. This isn't over, mark my words."

"Thanks, Polly, but I have to operate under the assumption that it is. My psychiatrist parents had lots to say about the research and literature concerning deathbed promises. It's not encouraging."

"It'd be one thing if he was at the end of his life, but he's young. That's just plain bizarre. I'm guessing that his wife must have been out of her mind at that point. How could you ask a loved one to keep a promise like that?"

"Well, she did, and it's done. What're we having for dinner, anyway? I'm starved."

The two friends hopped up and went to the kitchen. Lynn chopped and washed vegetables for a salad, and Polly grilled skewers of fish, shrimp, and vegetables, which she served over rice. After sitting with their plates, they toasted each other with seltzer.

Lynn took a bite. "Delicious! What kind of fish is this?"

"White fish, fresh caught today, according to the meat man at Valley Market."

"So, Poll, are you going to be okay working full-time? The last thing you need is to get overtired."

"Kev and I actually discussed that on the plane ride home. I was going to talk to you, then speak to the Morgans and Spark about maybe working half days just till the baby comes. I was, of course, obsessing about who would fill in for me and also worrying about you, but Leonora phoned this morning with what may be the solution to our problems."

"Uh-oh, please tell me she's not filling in for you."

Polly laughed. "No, no, nothing like that. Come on, you know me. Would I do that to you? Leonora's childhood friend, I can't remember her name... Anyway, this friend's daughter, Daisy, graduated with an early childhood degree from UC San Diego. She's been living at home with her folks in LA, and it sounds like they're driving each other bonkers."

"I know the feeling."

"Anyway, Daisy wanted to get out of LA and is interested in working at the Cottage. She can start full-time right after Labor Day. That's only a couple of weeks. I can hang on till then before going part-time just till baby comes. What do you think?"

"I think you should go part-time whenever you need to go part-time, as soon as next week. I'm assuming you'd work mornings and leave at noon? Between Rusty, Willow, and me, we can do afternoons."

"Are you sure?"

"Absolutely. And if this Daisy works out, maybe we'll be able to keep her on since we're in the middle of a major baby boom."

"That's true. Lorna Perez is pregnant too!"

"Geez, we'd better enjoy the last few days of our vacation, hadn't we?"

"Thanks, Lynn," Polly said, beaming. "And I'm sure things are going to work out for you and Gus."

"Yup, when we see pigs flying over the Gila."

"How about some ice cream for dessert? I went to Daily Scoop today and got four quarts! They have a new flavor, Swiss orange chocolate chip. It's to die for."

"I'm in," Lynn said, happy to be with her friend and colleague, her heart lighter than it had been for days.

CHAPTER 37

The weeks flew by. Emma's Dream closed for the season, and the Cottage went back to its regular routines. Daisy Springer arrived the Tuesday after Labor Day and proved to be a hard worker, eager to jump right in. She and Rusty had hit it off from day one. Redheads, hers more strawberry blonde than his, they were both freckle-faced and athletic. Daisy was a marathon runner, and Lynn predicted that soon she'd have Rusty running laps on the Loop Trail before school.

"Morning, ladies," Leonora said, two of her grandchildren in tow. "Maggie's gone down to Sonoita to pick up a couple of horses with Jeb, and my son's in Tucson with his dad, so I'm on baby duty. How's my girl doing?" she asked, gazing around.

"Daisy's not in yet," Polly said. "She starts at eight."

"Why don't you two ask her to start when you do? Get her used to the routines?"

"This works for now, thanks, Leonora, especially when we have our super helper," Lynn said, smiling at Emma, who had grabbed the children's circle mats and was setting them out.

"She's a true blessing, isn't she? As for that other one... Where'd he go?"

"He's getting his fort set up, Gran," Emma said.

Leonora rolled her eyes. "Of course he is. In preparation for the arrival of his partner in crime. How are you doing, Lynn? I'll bet you're anxious to have Gus back."

Lynn smiled. "I'm fine. It'll be great to have Dulcie and Cal back with us too."

Leonora gave her a quizzical look, but then shrugged. "I was hoping to catch Bethie. She's usually here by now, isn't she?"

"Lang usually drops Lily in the morning," Polly said, moving to the door to greet Lorna Perez and her daughter. "Morning, Christy!"

"Well then, I'll just give her a ring. Come on, Em. Lemme give your brother a kiss, and I'll drop you at school. Bye, ladies. Have a fabulous day!"

"Hey, ladies," Daisy Springer said, strolling in shortly after Leonora's departure. "I s'pose Aunt Nora was checkin' up on me?"

"Not really," Polly said. "She was dropping off the kids."

Lynn detected impatience in her friend's voice and gazed over at her. Polly was frowning as she gripped the side of a bookshelf near the doorway. "Hey, Poll, you okay?"

"Fine," she said, but she didn't look fine. Lynn saw that her free hand was shaking and all the color had drained from her face. This wasn't irritation at Daisy's flippant tone. Her colleague was in trouble. As Lynn watched, Polly swallowed hard and let go of the bookshelf.

"Rusty!" Lynn called. He was nearest to Polly, helping Ben with his fort, and he jumped up, catching Polly just as she began to fall.

"Here, put her on the sofa," Lynn called, scrambling to grab her phone. She dialed 911, then Kevin, all the while giving Daisy and Rusty directions to tend to the kids, get a cool cloth for Polly's head, and watch for the ambulance.

"Hey, Poll," she said softly as her friend's eyes fluttered open.

"What happened?"

"Looks like you fainted. The ambulance is on its way."

"That's not necessary. I'll be okay."

"Doctor's orders. He wants you to get checked out."

"Oh, Lynn," she said, gripping her friend's arm. "What if... I can't... It's too soon for the baby."

"Hey, you fainted, sweetie. Baby's gonna be fine. You too. You just need to get checked out."

The ambulance arrived at the same time as Kevin Larrabee. He ran in, cradling his wife in his arms, carrying her out. Lynn had sent the kids to the playground with Rusty and Daisy, so she helped settle Polly in the ambulance. "See you soon, sweetie," she said as Polly closed her eyes again.

"Thanks, Lynn," Kevin said, his eyes wild with worry. "I'll be back for Jasper."

"No worries. I'll take him home with me. Just let me know how she is."

Lynn was just closing up when Kevin called. "She's doing great, but they want to keep her overnight," he said. "How's Jasper?"

"Ben Morgan took him home. They're happy to have him spend the night with Benny, or I can pick him up and take him back with me."

"I'd like to stay with her," Kevin said.

"Of course you would."

"What do you think? About Jasper, I mean."

Despite her worry about Polly, Lynn smiled. "You know I love your son, but I guarantee he'll be happier at the Morgans than with dull old me. Want me to call them?"

"Would you, Lynn? Thanks, that'd be great."

"Tell her I love her," she said.

"Will do."

Lynn rang off and called the Morgans. Maggie answered. "How is she?"

"They're keeping her overnight. Kevin's with her. He asked if I'd call you about Jasper. I can come get him, but we all know where he'd be happiest."

"Of course, we'd be delighted to keep him. Benny will be thrilled. No worries. They're the same size. He can wear Ben's pj's and a clean set of clothes tomorrow. We'll get him to the Cottage."

"Thanks, Maggie."

"No worries. Night."

Lynn closed up, then decided to drive the short distance to Valley Hospital before heading home. Kevin was sitting beside a sleeping Polly when she peeked into the room. He spied her and stood, giving her a weary smile, indicating that they should step into the hallway.

"How's she doing?"

"Weak. Dr. Blake's concerned."

"And the baby?"

"Heartbeat's nice and strong. It's a girl, by the way. The nurse slipped when they were checking her. She didn't know we didn't know."

"What can I do? Would you like some supper? I can grab stuff from the cafeteria."

"Thanks, that'd be great. I'll eat anything."

Lynn hugged him. "She's stronger than you think. She'll be all right. Be back in a few."

Since Polly was still sleeping, they ate their cafeteria sandwiches in the empty lounge at the end of the hall. "What did Blake say?" Lynn asked.

"That she shouldn't get out of bed again until the baby comes."

"Then that's what she'll do."

"You know her. She'll fight us every step of the way. We're swamped with projects right now, but I can probably get time off. My crew can handle things."

"You know what the answer is, don't you?"

"Polly'll kill me if I call her."

"Then I will. Much as Phyllis drives me crazy, we need her now."

"Okay," he said, nodding. "Okay."

"She can stay with me at night to give you guys a break. It'll be fine."

"Thanks, Lynn."

Before she left the hospital, Lynn made a phone call, then popped into the room and found Polly groggy but awake. "Where's Jasper?" she asked.

"With the Morgans. They're happy to have him."

"What am I going to do?" Polly asked, gripping her arm.

"You're going to stay in bed, and people are going to take care of you."

"What people? Kevin's got so many projects right now that he can't see straight, and there's Jasper and the Cottage and…"

"Whoa, sweetie. We've got you covered." Lynn placed a hand on her forearm. "Now, don't get upset, but I called your mom. She's going to get a flight out tomorrow."

To Lynn's surprise, Polly nodded without protest, then closed her eyes. Kevin, who had been looking on, said, "They gave her a mild sedative. She's been doing this nodding off the past few hours."

"Probably just as well," Lynn said, hugging him. "I'm going to head out. Don't worry about Phyllis. I'll find a way to meet her plane or have someone do it. Once she gets here, she can use Polly's car to go back and forth from my place to yours."

"Thanks," he said. "You're a lifesaver."

Lynn smiled. *God, help us. I hope we can save Polly's life.*

CHAPTER 38

Kyle Morgan, resident vet in Horseshoe Crab Cove and vicinity, gently examined Crackers, who had come up lame at the end of a long ride the previous day. His Uncle Richard had hired him to consult until they decided whether to hire a resident veterinarian. As he ran fingers over the American Paint's knee, cannon, and pastern, the horse nickered softly.

"Hey," Gus said, just returning from town with supplies. "Good to see you. How's it going?"

Kyle looked up, grinning. "It's been crazy. I've treated every kind of animal from guinea pigs, rabbits, and hedgehogs to the usual dogs, cats, and horses. I've been a large animal vet since I graduated, so all these little critters have sent me back to the textbooks many times, I can tell you. Even had a monkey in last week."

"Is that legal?"

Kyle shrugged. "I suggested the little guy, a capuchin, might be happier in a zoo or sanctuary, but the owner seems pretty attached."

"Crazy what people do. How's he doing?" Gus asked, patting Crackers's flank.

"A mild sprain. Was he ridden hard?"

"Weezie Morgan had him out, so no telling. She's a good rider, but she likes speed. The trails around here are full of hazards. One minute, they're hard packed, the next, sand."

"Well, I'll wrap the pastern. That should help. No riding at all for at least a week, but he should be walked in the corral once or twice a day."

"Thanks. I've got a couple of things to do, but find me if you need me." Gus headed back into the barn.

As he stacked supplies and made inventory lists in the small room they used as an office, he ruminated on the return home. In less than two weeks, he would start the drive west to pick up the kids in Wyoming. Then it was back to the Valley and their new house out at Valley Stables. Although it was tough being away from the kids, he was glad he'd agreed to stay on a few more weeks. Things were coming together, trainers had been hired, and his assistant, Dennis, knew the ropes. Now all they needed was a head trainer. Management was handled by the Morgans, although the only one he ever saw was Weezie. Gail and Rich were infrequent visitors unless they needed something.

It had been good to stay and finish what he'd started. He'd been so busy, there'd been little time to think about life beyond Morgan's Run East or whatever they decided to call the new farm. Downtimes, when they came, his thoughts turned to Lynn. He missed her with an ache in his heart and loins that never completely left him. The sex had been incredible, but this kind, strong woman had touched him in ways he never thought possible after Lissie. Now he would have to face her and the hurt he'd caused. Then there would be questions from bosses and friends. *What a shit I'll be in their eyes,* he thought, leaning over his desk, head in hands.

"Hey, you okay, buddy?" Kyle said, startling him.

"Yeah...no...who knows."

"Guess you're eager to get home, right?"

"Yup."

"Long time to be away from your little guys."

"It has been."

"And I hear you and Lynn were getting pretty tight before you left. She's good people."

"Yes, she is, but about that... You'll probably hear soon enough. Got a few minutes?"

"Sure," Kyle said, pulling up a stool.

Gus surprised himself by relating most of the saga of the last few months, ending with her pregnancy, his revelation of his promise to Lissie, and the breakup with Lynn. "Fuckup, huh?" he said. When he met Kyle's eyes, he thought he glimpsed concern, not judgment.

"Hey, man, that sucks."

"Yup, it pretty much does."

"Do you still care about her?"

"I'm frickin' crazy about her. You know, I was with my wife from the time we were kids. We grew up together, and there was basically no one else. Then I met Lynn, and I've felt things I've never felt before. I'm not just talking about sex either, although it is pretty amazing. Please don't repeat that or any of this, man. I'm not one to kiss and tell."

Kyle nodded. "No worries. You're in a bind, huh?"

"Don't s'pose you have any advice? I sure hate to go back to the Valley and hurt Lynn more by my presence. Of course I'm thrilled about the baby, even if I can't tell her or be there for her the way she wants."

"Maybe she'll need a friend?"

"Doubt that'll be me," Gus said morosely.

"Don't take this wrong, but have you ever talked to anyone about the whole promise thing? Like a therapist?"

"No. I went to grief counseling and a grief support group for a while. I've been thinking about trying to find something like that when I get back. Maybe I need a tune-up."

"My family's big on therapists. There's a wonderful one in Saguaro, Haley Alvarez. You could look her up when you get back. Harriet swears by her woman here too. Elise something. I could get her name if you like?"

"Thanks," Gus said. "If you think of it, text me. I'll try anything to get my head on straight so I don't go home and make things ten times worse."

"I hear you, man. Harriet's teaching, but I'll ask her tonight."

"Thanks, man," Gus said, walking Kyle to his truck. "So this is a big change for you, living out here?"

"Don't tell my folks, 'cause I love 'em, but I prefer the East Coast to the Valley. This feels like home. Of course, Harriet's here, and wherever she is, that's home for me."

"You're lucky."

"Don't I know it. Will be in touch later." Kyle tipped his hat and was gone.

CHAPTER 39

The days at the Cottage went by without Polly. Lynn missed her terribly. With Daisy and Rusty full-time, they were managing well, but it wasn't the same. She and Polly had built the Cottage from scratch, planning every detail of the educational space and programs. Leonora Morgan had lent a decorating hand, but it was their school, and they were both so proud of it. *What if something happens and she can't come back?* Lynn thought numerous times throughout each day. The thought left her feeling cold and lonely. Every evening, she would stop by Polly and Kevin's to say hello. Sometimes on the weekends, she'd visit with Polly while Kevin and Jasper had an outing or Phyllis needed to run errands. Polly always knew what to say to cheer her up.

"It's gonna be okay, I bet," she said one evening as the two friends sat by the fire. The weather had turned uncharacteristically cold for the end of September, and Kevin had lit the fire before taking Jasper to the movies. They were meeting the Morgan family so that the two boys could enjoy the newest superhero movie together. Phyllis had gone back to Lynn's to take a bath.

"It'll be what it'll be," Lynn said, stretching out. "I'm sure we can be friendly and professional. It'll be weird at first, but I can handle it."

"You can totally handle it, but can he?"

"It's his promise and his mess," she said. "There, I've said it. I'm pissed."

"Does he know that?"

"No, but what's the use? It won't change anything. Just make things awkward."

"I thought I might get Mom to drive me down to visit Monday," Polly said. "I miss you and the kids."

"We miss you, but that might not be a good idea. They've all got colds, and you don't need that."

"Well... Maybe later in the week. I can wear rubber gloves. I'm going stir-crazy here."

"Only a few more weeks, right?"

"Baby's not due till the end of October. I'm hoping to hang on to her until then so she'll be healthy."

"So, enjoy the rest. It'll be the last until she's beyond the teenage years."

Polly smiled, reaching over to squeeze her hand. "I'm so glad we're having these babies together. It'll be so much fun watching them grow up together."

Lynn nodded. "It's gonna be cool."

"Lynn, if something happens... If I don't...you know—"

"Hey, hey, where's that coming from?"

"Please let me finish. If something happens to me, you'll look after Kev and the kids for me, won't you? I mean, I would hope he'd find a wonderful woman to marry, and I've made it clear to him that that's what I want. But just in case that takes a while, promise me you'll look after them."

"You know that's not going to be necessary, sweetie." *Please, God, don't let it be necessary!*

"Please, Lynn! Please promise."

Lynn squeezed her hand. "Of course, you got it."

"Thank you," Polly said, smiling as she let out a long sigh.

∼

"Hello, welcome," Elise Nolan said, stepping aside to allow Gus to enter her small, comfortable office.

"Thanks so much for seeing me on such short notice."

"Of course. Would you like something to drink? Water? Tea? Coffee? A soft drink or seltzer?"

"Water would be great, thanks."

The therapist opened a small refrigerator and brought out two bottles of water, one of which she handed to him. "Sit, please," she said, indicating one of the overstuffed chairs. She took the other, sat, and opened her water, taking a swallow. A long-distance runner according to Kyle, her short dark hair was cropped and spiky and she wore leggings, a long-sleeved tee and clogs, which she let slide onto the floor as she crossed her legs under her.

"Now then, how can I help?"

"Could I just kind of tell the whole story?" he asked.

"Please." Her eyes were warm and encouraging.

When he finished, he said, "That's it. I've hurt someone I care very deeply about and yet I feel a loyalty to a woman who gave her life for our son. I literally have no idea what to do."

"Hmm," Elise said, shifting slightly in her chair. "What do you want to do?"

"I want to be with Lynn. I love her. But I made a promise to Lissie that I cannot break."

"Why is that?"

"I believe in keeping promises."

"I do too, but keeping promises is, perhaps, something we reserve for the living?"

Gus shrugged. "You've got me there. All I know is that my wife was dying, but very clear."

"Yes."

"How does this work? Do you give advice?"

"I prefer not to advise but to provide a listening space where my clients can make their own decisions."

"Have you had clients who have made promises like this? The leader of my bereavement group called them deathbed promises."

"I have known people, yes."

"What did they do?"

"Everyone makes different choices."

"So some people break promises like this?"

Elise paused, sipping her water, pensive for a minute or two before responding. "I wonder if it's helpful to look at them as broken?"

"What else would it be? I mean, technically I've already broken part of my promise 'cause Lynn's going to have our baby. I can't stop her and wouldn't want to if I could."

"That seems a little gray to me," she said, setting her water bottle on the table. "Can you really characterize what's happened as breaking a promise? It sounds like the pregnancy was unexpected, was it not?"

"Completely. Lynn was always adamant about protection."

"So the pregnancy is an unexpected joy? Disappointment? Accident? Catastrophe? How would you describe it? Would you characterize is as an intentional action to break a promise?"

"No to the last. Unexpected for sure. Happy, because I love kids and I know Lynn will be a terrific mother."

"So is it fair to say that the baby is not a deliberate act to break a promise?"

He nodded. "When you think about it, no, it doesn't seem to fit."

"But it happened, and it does go against your deceased wife's wishes."

"Yes."

"Making peace with that may be a constructive first step. Then making peace with whether you want to be involved in this child's life in any way. That is, if Lynn is agreeable."

"Yes. What about the rest?"

"That's for you to decide, Gus. It doesn't sound as if you intended to break your promise to Lissie in falling in love with Lynn. It happened. It's your present-day reality. What you do or don't do with that realization is up to you."

He smiled. "It makes perfect sense talking about it now. It's a shame I'm leaving soon and can't come back."

"Maybe," she said, softly, "but from where I'm sitting, you don't need me. You need Lynn. You guys together can decide what makes sense going forward. Maybe friends? Maybe more? You could take things slow and see where they lead."

As Gus walked out onto the sidewalk in Horseshoe Crab Cove, the afternoon shone brightly, and he shielded his eyes. *Thank you, Elise Nolan,* he thought, his mind and body calmer than they'd been in many weeks.

CHAPTER 40

"That's one cute dad," Daisy said as she passed through to the kitchen with Dulcie's and Cal's lunch boxes. Lynn gulped, spying the familiar bags. She dried her hands, took a deep breath, and stepped into the main room, where Gus was helping Cal out of his jacket. He looked up and spied her, smiling. "Hey, we're back."

"So you are," Lynn said, opening her arms to Dulcie, who ran to greet her. "Hey, sweetie, we missed you! Did you have fun with Grandma and Grandpa and Aunt Laurie?"

Dulcie nodded, resting her head against Lynn's shoulder.

"I bet they were sad to see you go."

The child nodded again, then whispered, "We have a new house."

"I heard about that. Is it nice?"

Dulcie beamed. "And there are horses."

Lynn looked up at Gus. "So you're all moved in?"

"Well, boxes everywhere, but it's gonna be great. We'll have to get Lynn out to see it, won't we, Dulce?"

As Dulcie ran off to join the children in the block room, he stood next to Lynn. "Didn't mean to presume, but I hope we can... That we will... Can be friends?"

"Glad to have you back."

"How are you feeling?"

"Fine. I feel fine," she said, unwilling to go into detail. It somehow felt too intimate, too personal. "We have a new teacher. Daisy. And you remember Rusty, right?"

"Yup, hey, Rusty," he called, smiling as he watched him building a tall tower with the kids.

"Polly's on bed rest till the baby comes, so we may hire someone else part-time soon. Between the ranch and the farm, we're experiencing a baby boom around here," she said as the door opened and Lang Dillon stepped in with his daughter in his arms.

"Morning, Lily!" Lynn called as Gus stowed his kids' things and prepared to leave.

"Have a great day," Gus said, nodding to Lang and then catching Lynn's eye.

She waved, then turned to chat with Lang.

As he drove to work, Gus mused on the roller-coaster week that had brought him home to the Valley. He had spent a few days with his family in Jackson Hole before packing up for the drive south.

During the time with his parents, he'd visited Lissie's grave. As he sat on a nearby bench, talking to the girl he'd known for most of his life, he was startled by a tap on his shoulder. "Talkin' with my girl, are you?"

"Jim," he said, standing in surprise, shaking the older man's hand. He hadn't seen Lissie's dad for several years, mostly because Jim always traveled for work and was frequently out of town when Gus visited. "Good to see you."

"You too, Gus." Like his daughters, Jim Olsen was short and slender, his dark brown hair peppered with gray and thinning on top. He had Lissie's pale brown eyes and her smile.

"It's been a while."

"Too long, son. Say, Jeannie and I had more fun with the kids this summer. That Cal's a pistol and Dulcie's my little princess. Your folks were real good about sharing 'em too. We had 'em over once or twice a week."

"So I heard. They're good kids."

"You've done well with them, Gus. It's not easy being mother and father to kids, but somehow, you do it."

"You certainly did a great job." Jim's wife had died when Lissie was five, so the two men had single parenting in common.

"Yeah, well, kids are kids. You love 'em and give 'em shelter and food, and they turn out fine. Grandparents help. My parents sure pitched in with my girls. A shame you aren't livin' closer."

"Yeah, I'm sorry about the distance. We do have lots of help and support in the Valley. It's a pretty incredible place."

"I'd like to visit one day."

"Anytime."

"I have a regular run down to Prescott. There are two clients there. Maybe next time I'm in the area?" Jim's company sold specialized machinery and tools to farms all over the country and sometimes overseas.

"That'd be great. The kids would love it, and we've got a big house now."

"You know, the one thing I did wrong, son? I never found another gal after my Raelynn. She was my sweetheart, like Lissie was yours. I should've looked harder. It's lonely."

"But what about Sally and Cora and the others?" To the consternation of his daughters, Jim had had a succession of lady friends over the years.

"Not the same. I wasn't looking for long-term in those days, so I intentionally chose ladies I knew wouldn't stay around. Big mistake."

"It's never too late," Gus said.

"Maybe, but what about you? I hear you have a gal."

"Lynn. She's just a friend."

"Not according to Jeannie. Says you kicked her to the curb for this gal. Must be serious."

"It is or was. I made a mistake getting involved, after my promise to Lissie. She... Lynn... She's terrific. She deserves more."

His father-in-law patted his shoulder. "Things have a way of working themselves out, son. Don't give up the ghost yet. Hey, wanta grab a cup of coffee and a donut?"

"I can't. I promised the kids we'd go fishing. I'm already late. You're welcome to join us, if you like."

"Thanks, but I'll take a rain check. Good fishing in that valley of yours?"

"Yup."

"Then count me in on my next visit. Good to see you, son."

As Gus headed to the truck, he reflected on his words to Jim. *Friends. Is that true? Would that ever work?* He'd given a lot of thought to his conversation with Elise Nolan. He wasn't sure of a lot of things, but he knew he couldn't allow Lynn to walk out of his life, and he was pretty sure that he wanted to raise his children, *all three of them,* in the beautiful valley that already felt like home.

CHAPTER 41

After several invitations, Lynn finally agreed to come out to Valley Stables. How could she refuse when Dulcie asked every day, "When are you coming to see our new house?" On a sunny Saturday, she headed north to Valley Stables in the late morning. She stopped on her way to pick up lunch things and to see Polly, and had made plans to come back that evening to visit with her while Kevin and Jasper went to dinner at the Morgans'. Phyllis had been invited to dinner by the elder Morgans at their club, so it would be a good chance for Lynn and Polly to catch up.

As she turned off the main road onto the farm's mile-long drive, she wondered if this was a good idea. Not only was it hard to be around Gus with her conflicted feelings, she wasn't feeling all that well and had been having morning sickness the past few days. She had stopped at the café in town to pick up sandwiches, and now she wasn't sure she'd be able to eat one.

As she drove into the farm proper, the land opened up, and one could see for miles in all directions. Gus's place was to the south, down a short drive. The house had been built for the farm manager, but Tom Jacobi had insisted they give it to Gus since he was a bachelor and didn't need a large three-bedroom house. He was happy living in one of the Morgan's Run cabins. The next phase of building at Valley Stables included two additional houses, one for Tom and the other for the resident vet, Patty Turner, but Ben and Leonora assured Tom that he was welcome to stay in the cabin forever.

The three were waiting in the yard as she drove in, the kids jumping up and down with excitement. As she parked, she marveled at the beauty of Ben Morgan and Spark Foster's dream, now reality. It had been a while since she'd been to Valley Stables and she was in awe. Miles of green grass, two racetracks, a series of barns, stables, bunkhouses, and corrals were visible from the manager's house, perched as it was on a rise. The foundations for several other buildings were visible to the south and west.

"Wow!" she said, hopping out of the car. "This is amazing."

Gus smiled. "This is what millions and the will of two movers and shakers will get you."

"They are incredible, aren't they?"

"Yup. Come on, the kids are dying to show you around."

A sturdy, well-built house in the style of many western homes, it had a wide porch that circled the entire house, affording magnificent views of the valley and mountains to the east and west. The living room was sparsely furnished, with many boxes piled to one side. A beautiful kitchen with island, granite counters, and burnished cherry cabinets had a sunny breakfast nook with window seats that opened into a family room with a stone fireplace. The master bedroom was down a short hallway, and there were two bedrooms and a bath upstairs. Boxes were everywhere as they made their way from room to room.

"This is beautiful, you guys," Lynn said. "What a great spot. I'd be happy to help unpack a little after lunch, if you'd like."

"I can't ask you to do that," he said.

"You didn't ask, I offered," she said, brushing by him to join the children. With every breath, she was conscious of him and his nearness. *Keep your distance, girl,* she told herself as they headed to the kitchen to prepare lunch.

"It's pretty warm out. Shall we eat out back? The kids love it out there."

As they sat on the porch watching Cal and Dulcie chase each other, rolling around on the verdant Kentucky bluegrass, she said, "What a place."

"Yeah, it's prey cool. I'm going into Tucson next week to order a swing set for 'em. Thanks for coming, Lynn. It means a lot to the kids and me."

"Honestly, it feels a little weird, but I'm glad I came, and I'm happy to help with the unpacking. Why don't I tackle the kids' rooms or the kitchen for a few hours?"

"Are you sure?"

"Yes," she said, softly, turning to him with a shy smile. "We have to get through this somehow, and friends seems like a good start, don't you think?"

"You are the most amazing person I know," he said, reaching out to take her hand.

His touch seared into her skin, and Lynn quickly withdrew her hand and stood up. Close proximity was going to be tricky when every fiber of her being longed for him. "What do you say? Shall we get cracking?"

Gus called the kids, and they all went in. "I'm sorry I did that," he whispered as the kids ran upstairs. "I want... I miss...oh, forget it. I'm a shit, and that's all that needs to be said."

She gazed over at him. The man she knew and loved was a mess, his beautiful eyes sad. "It's fine. Don't beat yourself up. Point me in the right direction, and let's get to work. Okay?" she said, patting his shoulder.

They spent the afternoon unpacking and breaking down countless boxes. Within a short time, the kitchen was nearly unpacked except for boxes of what Gus had labeled "Wedding China." Lynn decided to let him deal with those, and she headed upstairs. By four thirty, the children's rooms were fully settled, books and toys in the beautiful built-in bookshelves that lined their walls. Cal toddled from room to room as Dulcie played with toys she hadn't seen in three months.

"What do you think, Dulcie?" Lynn asked as she hung the last of four framed pictures on her wall, then placed several family photos on the child's bedside table. "Is this where you'd like these?"

Dulcie nodded. "I have one more over here," she said, bringing a silver-framed photo of her mother holding her. "I say good night to Mommy, so she has to be there too."

"That's a beautiful picture of two beautiful girls," Lynn said, hugging her. Dulcie leaned against her, wrapping her arms around her.

"Hey, sweetie, are you okay?"

"Are you gonna be our new mommy?"

Lynn knelt beside her, taking her tiny hands in her own. "Your daddy and I are really good friends, honey, and we both love you."

At that moment, Cal burst in, running for the shelf where his sister had just arranged her dolls. "No!" Dulcie screamed as Lynn intercepted Cal and scooped him up.

"Hey, guys, I've gotta get going."

"You're not staying for supper?" Dulcie said.

"Can't tonight, sweetie. I'm taking care of Polly, and she's expecting me soon."

As she carried Cal down the stairs, Lynn felt a small pang in her side and grimaced. Gus spied her and grabbed the toddler from her arms. "What's wrong? Are you okay?"

"Fine, just a twinge," she said, sitting in one of the living room chairs.

"Geez, Lynn, what an idiot I was to let you do this in your condition." He knelt beside her, eyes full of concern, Cal still in his arms. "Can I get you something?"

"No, really, Gus. I'm fine. I do have to get going, though, 'cause I'm on Polly duty tonight."

"Why didn't you say so?"

"Because I've been having fun here," she said, smiling as Dulcie came up behind them. "Wait'll you see Dulcie's room. It's pretty cool, isn't it?" She winked at the child.

"Dulcie," he said, "can you take your brother to the kitchen and get him a juice? Thanks, sweetheart."

"Here, I'll walk you out," he said, offering his hand, which she ignored.

At the car, he said, "Thanks again. It was great having you here, and I hope we can do it again soon."

"Happy to help."

"You sure you're okay?"

"Absolutely. Gus, Dulcie seems a bit confused right now. She just asked me if I was going to be her mommy, so you might want to chat with her and explain that we're just friends. I don't want to disappoint her or hurt her feelings."

"Lynn... I am so sorry... I've made a shit awful mess out of something that was really amazing."

She reached over and touched his arm. "I've gotta go. Polly's expecting me. Have a great night."

With that, she hopped into her car and started off, not daring to look back. Tears clouded her vision as she drove down the farm drive, and she pulled over, scrambling around for a tissue. *This friends thing is going to be agony, especially since I love him more every time I see him.*

CHAPTER 42

Cal in bed asleep, Gus read Dulcie one of her current favorite stories, *The Patchwork Cat*. When he closed the book, he hugged her close. "Hey, sweetie, Lynn told me that you were wondering if she was going to be your mommy. Is that right?"

She nodded, gazing over at the photo of her and her mother.

"I know you'd like that, sweetie, but right now, Lynn and I are friends."

"But I saw you kissing before we left for Gramma's."

"I know... That was confusing."

"Do you love her?"

"Yes."

"Why can't she be our mommy, then?"

"Sweetie, it's complicated right now. I want to do the best thing for you, Cal, and Lynn, and I'm not sure what that is, so we decided to be friends."

"Is it 'cause you still love Mommy?"

"I will always love Mommy, Dulce. That's never going to change. But it's possible to love lots of people. We're going to figure it out, I promise, but for now, Lynn's a really good friend of mine and yours, and that's a good thing, right?"

Dulcie nodded, then whispered, "Good night, Mommy," before turning to hug and kiss him. "Night, baby."

"Night, Daddy."

"So this is really nice, isn't it?" Lynn said, stretching out, her feet on the coffee table. "It's been a while since we had a girls' night." She looked over, smiling, and found Polly frowning, hand on her stomach. Instantly, Lynn sat up. "Hey, Poll, you okay?"

"Yes, fine. I guess that pizza didn't agree with me."

"You sure?"

"Yes. Tell me more about what's been happening with you at the Cottage, with Gus. All of it."

Lynn began describing the past few weeks, rambling on, aware that Polly was only half listening. Something was wrong, and her friend was trying valiantly to hide it. Finally, she stopped. "Polly Larrabee, if you don't tell me right now what's wrong, I'm going to bundle you right out to my car and take you to the hospital."

"Actually, that would be good," Polly said, her voice weak. "Grab my phone, would you? Dr. Blake's number is there, and my OB. Call Kevin and my mom too." No sooner were the words out of her mouth than Polly fainted.

Lynn called 911, then the others. The ambulance arrived within minutes and they raced to the hospital, Lynn holding her friend's hand as they took her vitals and placed an oxygen mask over Polly's face. *Oh please, God, let us make it,* she thought, gazing down at the pale face.

They reached Valley Hospital in record time, and Lynn heard one of the EMTs say, "She's really weak. She needs a cardiologist and fast."

As they wheeled Polly inside, Kevin's truck flew in the drive, and he jumped out. "Where is she?"

"Just inside. Thank God you're here. You go. Give me your keys, and I'll move the truck."

Kevin's eyes were wild as he gazed at her. "Jesus, why did I leave her? It's bad, isn't it?"

Lynn placed her hand on his arm. "She's here, and she's in good hands. Go, I'll be right in."

As she hurried back from the parking lot, she spied Mark Blake running in a side door reserved for hospital staff. *Thank God,* she thought, heading into the bright lights of the emergency room.

When she reached the second floor, Lynn was relieved to spy Phyllis Granger. Beside her, Kevin paced and Spark Foster stood quietly. "Phyllis, so glad you got here so quickly."

"Thanks to Spark," she said, hugging Lynn.

"Why won't they let me see her?" Kevin said to no one in particular. His eyes were bloodshot, and it was clear he'd been crying.

"They'll be out once they get her assessed and stable," Phyllis said, her voice remarkably calm and strong.

Lynn was about to ask if people wanted food or drink when Mark Blake came into the lounge, a short, bespectacled woman at his side. "Hello, folks, this is Dr. Gannon, the obstetrician on call tonight. So far we've been unable to reach Polly's doctor, who's on vacation this week."

"On vacation, Jesus Christ," Kevin said, "What about other doctors from the practice?"

"I requested Dr. Gannon," Blake said, his voice calm and quiet. "With your permission, she's the one I would like to deliver the baby."

"Deliver the baby?" Kevin said. "She's not due for three weeks."

Mark Blake's kind eyes regarded the group for a few seconds before he turned to Kevin. "Mr. Larrabee, Kevin, we need to deliver this baby now. Tonight. Polly's heart is very weak, and the baby's putting too much strain on her body. Dr. Gannon concurs."

"What does Polly say? Is she awake? Can I see her?"

"You can see her for a minute, but she's groggy and won't make any sense."

"Why?"

"Because she's very weak."

Dr. Gannon cleared her throat and spoke softly, her voice rich and deep. "Mr. Larrabee, your wife cannot deliver vaginally in her condition. We need to do an emergency C-section, and we need your permission. Dr. Blake will be with me the whole time."

Phyllis stepped forward. "May we both see her? Very quickly, before you go ahead?"

"Yes, of course. I do have forms."

"I want to see her first, then I'll sign anything you want," Kevin said as they followed the doctors out of the room.

When they were gone, Lynn collapsed onto a vinyl chair, her vision blurry, her stomach queasy. Spark came to her side. "Hey, darlin', you don't look well. Can I get you something?"

"I feel a little woozy, that's all," she murmured through the fog as Spark pulled out his phone and began talking. Within a minute, a stretcher appeared, and nurses helped her to lie down.

"I want a doctor for her, now," Spark said. "Is there someone available? She's with child as well."

Surprised, Lynn looked at him, then thought, *Of course the Morgans would have told him. He should know.* As they wheeled her out, she wondered if her employers had also told Spark who the baby's father was. She hated to have Gus vilified if things didn't work out between them, but what could she do?

In three strides, Spark caught up to the stretcher. "Is there anyone I can call for you, darlin'?"

"Not yet. Let's see how I am," she said. "Thanks, Spark."

"Don't you worry about a thing. I'll keep 'em on their toes," he said.

Lynn gave him a wan smile as they disappeared through double doors. Suddenly exhausted, she closed her eyes.

CHAPTER 43

"Ms. Manguilli?" a voice said as someone touched her arm.

Lynn's first thought was of Polly, and she sat up. "How is she?"

"The baby's fine," the young physician said. "You're fine too, just overtired, I'd guess. I'm Dr. Wilkins, an OB resident. Mr. Foster out there has requested a doctor from Tucson. She should be here soon."

Lynn smiled at the slender blond doctor who looked about twelve. "Don't take it personally. This is what he does."

"So I've been told."

"And I would guess his dear friends the Morgans will be swooping in soon."

He grinned. "Already here."

"I'm sorry. I'm fine. Really. I was asking about my friend, Polly Larrabee. She's having an emergency C-section."

Wilkins's face turned grave. "I think she's still in the OR."

Lynn grasped his arm. "Please tell me if you know anything."

"I don't, but I can check. Hang tight, and your other doc should be in soon."

"This is ridiculous," Lynn said, starting to rise, then realized she was in a johnny. "Where are my clothes?"

"They're in the closet, I expect," he said, placing his hands gently on her shoulders. "Let's keep you in bed. I'll check on your friend and have a nurse come in and help you dress as soon as you get your second opinion."

Fuming, Lynn surrendered to the inevitable and lay back, closing her eyes. She opened them a few minutes later when someone touched her arm. Expecting to see the Tucson doctor, she was shocked to find Gus staring down at her, his eyes full of concern. "Oh!" she said, sitting up, pulling the johnny around her. "How did you...? I mean who...?"

"Spark called."

"What about the kids? Who's with them?"

"No worries. One of the crew's at the house. They were asleep. He's a good guy, and they know him."

"Gus, this isn't necessary. You should be with them in the new house and all."

"I think it is," he said quietly. "And I intend to stay until I'm sure you're okay."

"I'm fine. Have you heard anything about Polly?"

He shook his head. "I came straight up here."

"I'm so worried about her. She was white as a ghost and so weak."

The door opened, and a tall woman with short salt-and-pepper hair and deep gray eyes stepped in. "Hello, I'm May Tillson from Tucson. Your friend called and asked me to check in on you."

"Hello, Dr. Tillson," Lynn said. "This is totally unnecessary."

"Perhaps, but since I'm here, why don't I take a peek? Is this your husband?"

"No, he's a friend."

Gus stood. "I'm Gus, Gus Casey. Glad you're here. I'll just wait outside."

As he headed for the door, Lynn felt the now familiar chill run through her. "Please check on Polly, please!" she cried before turning her attention to Dr. Tillson.

Dr. Tillson took her time examining Lynn, asking many questions. Finally, she said. "You're in great shape except for perhaps being a little run-down. Have you been taking care of yourself? Taking prenatal vitamins?"

"Yes to the vitamins. I direct an infant-toddler program, and my codirector is the woman undergoing an emergency C-section as we speak. She's been out on bed rest for a number of weeks, so it's been a little more hectic than usual. And I probably did too much today helping a friend unpack his moving boxes."

"Gus?"

"Yes. He has two lively preschoolers who were helping us too."

"And he's the father of your baby, if I'm not mistaken."

"How did you...? Did someone say?"

The doctor smiled. "When two people have the connection you two have, it's obvious that there's more to the relationship. Also, he is here with you tonight."

"Not at my request," Lynn said, then realized that sounded harsh. "But you're right, he's been more than a friend, but it's complicated. And yes, he's the baby's father."

"Well, this little baby is fine, and so are you."

"Can I go home, then?"

"I'll have the nurse come and help you dress."

"Did you hear anything about my friend on your way in?"

May Tillson smiled, patting her hand.

"No, but you sit tight. I'm sure there'll be news soon. Now, to give my report to the bosses."

"Sorry."

"Don't be. They're delightful, and I'm getting two helicopter rides in one night."

"Oh Lord," Lynn said as the tall physician closed the door behind herself.

Almost immediately, Gus reappeared. "Hey, sounds like you're okay?"

"So what did you find out?"

"The baby's been born. A little girl. She's tiny and on a respirator, but they're optimistic."

"And?"

"The cardiologist is with Polly, monitoring her. She's struggling right now."

"Oh, Gus," she cried as he stepped forward and folded her into his strong arms. He held her as Lynn sobbed for her dearest friend. "I'm so frightened."

"I know, my girl, I know," he said, holding her. "Your Polly's a fighter, and she's been in this kind of situation before, according to her mom. They say the next twelve hours will tell."

Ten minutes later, Gus was still sitting on the edge of the bed, holding her when the nurse appeared. "Ready to get dressed, Ms. Manguilli?"

Gus stood and released her. "I'll be right outside." He kissed the top of her head and withdrew.

CHAPTER 44

On tottery legs and leaning on Gus's arm, Lynn walked down the hall to join the others. Kevin was in the neonatal unit with their daughter, as yet unnamed, and Polly was unconscious but holding her own. Phyllis sat in the lounge staring into space, Spark beside her. Leonora had gone to get food and drinks. Ben Senior gave Lynn a hug. "Here, sit, darlin'. Nora'll be back soon with some snacks."

Leonora was just distributing hot drinks and snacks when Mark Blake stepped into the lounge. "Hey, folks, I'm looking for Kevin."

"He's up with the baby," Spark said, stepping forward with Phyllis, who appeared to be leaning heavily on his arm.

"Okay, I'll find him."

"How is she?" Phyllis asked. "My husband's on his way. Will she be... Is she going to... How is she?"

"Her heart's okay, but her body's had a pretty major shock. People with VSD have trouble with any extra stresses on the body, and I don't have to tell the women in the room that pregnancy and the birth of a baby are major stressors. Polly's strong in spirit, but her body's fragile. She's a fighter, though. I'll stay with her through the night. I thought Kevin might like to join me."

"I'm sure he would," Phyllis said, tears in her eyes.

"And you too, Mom," the doctor said. "I'm pretty sure she'd want you there. Let's go find Kevin."

Spark delivered Phyllis to Mark Blake's arm. "Don't you worry about your husband. My guy's at the airport. He'll bring Perris here. We'll let you know as soon as he arrives."

"Thank you, dear Spark," she said, her usually robust voice reedy and weak.

When they departed, Leonora turned to Lynn. "Can one of us take you home, honey?"

"I'm staying," Lynn said.

"No, you're not," Gus said, his voice quiet but firm. "I'll take her."

To Lynn's relief, the drive home was quiet. When they arrived at the condo, he ran around to help her out of the car. "Gus, I'm fine, really. No need to treat me like an invalid."

He ignored her and took hold of her arm, guiding her to the door. Once inside, he helped her with her sweater, then walked her to the bedroom. Their nearness had them both on edge, but there was also comfort and warmth that both had missed. He helped her out of her clothes and into one of the long T-shirts she used as pajamas. His touch warmed her, and she leaned against him, closing her eyes for a few seconds. *So much we've lost. How I miss you, Gus Casey.* Suddenly shaking herself, she stepped back. "Thanks, that's fine. I'll just go wash up."

Gus sat in a chair, watching the closed bathroom door, determined to see her settled in bed before he departed. Those moments in the hospital holding her and these last few minutes were precious, the first peaceful moments he'd had for many weeks. *What a fool I've been.*

He smiled as Lynn emerged. "Here you go." He moved to the bed and turned back the covers.

"Gus, this is really not necessary," she said as she slipped under the sheets.

"I think it is. Now, can I get you anything?"

"No, I'm fine. Will be good to get some sleep. So glad tomorrow's Sunday."

"And maybe you should take a couple of days off. From what I've seen, Rusty and Daisy are doing great, and they can get some part-timers from town."

"Don't be ridiculous. I'm fine, just scared to death about Polly."

"She's gonna pull through, you'll see," he said, remembering his recent conversation with Jim Olsen and the loss of two young mothers. *Is Polly to be another young mom gone?*

As Lynn's eyes fluttered and closed, he bent down and kissed her forehead. "Sleep well, my love," he whispered, then turned out the light and slipped from the room.

Lynn rolled over. Despite her worry about Polly, she had a smile on her face.

CHAPTER 45

Her faintness of the previous evening forgotten, Lynn hopped out of bed. After a quick shower, she dressed, then grabbed a muffin and coffee from the café in town on her way to the hospital. Kevin had texted that Polly was doing a little better, and Lynn wanted to see her, if possible, or at least check in. When she arrived, she found Spark and Leonora in the lounge on Polly's floor. "How's she doing?" Lynn asked, hugging each of them in turn.

"No change, or at least we haven't heard from anyone since we arrived," Leonora said. "I made Ben stay home. I wanted to come in to relieve Spark, but the man just won't go."

Spark grinned. "This big ole recliner got me plenty of shut-eye, and Aria just brought in a basket of food, so I'm all set. Anyone hungry?"

"Carmela made an equally large basket, so there's plenty," Leonora said.

"Thanks, but I just had a muffin," Lynn said. "Has her dad arrived?"

"On the way now with Jimmy," Spark said, referring to one of his drivers.

"How are *you* feeling, honey?" Leonora asked, coming to sit beside her.

"I feel great, thanks. Just needed a good night's sleep. I'd really like to see her."

Spark stood. "Let's see what I can find out." He stepped out of the room, returning several minutes later. He met Lynn's eyes. "She's awake, and she'd like to see you."

"Praise the Lord," Leonora said.

Still ashen and weak, Polly was sitting up, Kevin on one side of her, her mother on the other. "Hi, sweetie," Lynn said.

"Hey," Polly said. "You just missed Julia Perris Larrabee. They just wheeled her away."

"I'll go take a peek later. Right now, I'm just so glad to see *you*." She leaned over the bed and hugged her friend's frail shoulders. "You gave us quite a scare, Polly Larrabee."

"I know, I'm sorry. And poor Dad, who hates to fly, is on his way too."

Lynn gazed around the room. Phyllis and Kevin looked exhausted but happy. "Did you guys get any sleep?"

Phyllis smiled. "They've been wheeled away, but Spark somehow managed to have two gigantic recliners put in this tiny room, complete with down comforters. You should have seen us. Poor Dr. Blake could barely get to Polly."

Lynn smiled. "What? Spark didn't order him a chair too?"

"Oh, Lynn, she's so beautiful. I can't wait for you to meet her!"

"She is a beauty," Kevin said. "Just like her mom." He held Polly's hand, gently massaging the alabaster skin.

They chatted awhile until Perris Granger arrived, then Lynn said her hellos and goodbyes. Kevin walked out with her to the neonatal ward. "There she is," he said proudly, pointing to the impossibly tiny pink bundle. "They've taken her off the respirator, and she's breathing on her own. Polly is determined to breast feed, but they're holding off till she's a little stronger. We did give her a bottle this morning."

"Oh, Kev, she's gorgeous. I can't wait to hold her."

"Want me to ask 'em? We can suit up and go in."

A few minutes later, Julia in her arms, Lynn's eyes filled with tears.

"I know," he said, standing beside her. "Life is precious, isn't it? We almost lost both of 'em. I don't know what I'd do."

"But they're fine, aren't you, sweet Julia?" she said, cooing at the infant. "When can they come home?"

"They'd like to keep Julia for a few days. They figure Polly can go home on bed rest tomorrow, but she's probably gonna want to stay with the baby."

"I don't blame her. What a sweet girl she is."

"Yup."

"So happy for you, Kev. How's Jasper? Do you want me to pick him up from the Morgans'?"

"Maggie's gonna bring him in later. He'll go home with me or the Grangers. Phyllis insists she wants to sleep on the couch and watch Jasper, but I'm trying to convince her to keep staying at your place with Perris."

"I can help with that," Lynn said. "I'll talk to them before I leave."

They chatted awhile longer, then went back to Polly's room. Lynn chatted briefly with Perris Granger in the hall, and he said, "No worries, I'll take care of Grandma." As he hugged Lynn, he added, "I understand that congratulations are in order for you too?"

"Yes."

"Phyllis and I couldn't be happier. Now you girls will be mommas together, compare notes and all."

"Thanks, Perris. I'm going to take off, but please call if you need a ride or anything."

"I believe we have our chauffeur at the ready day and night, and we have Polly's car at the house, so we're all set."

"I'm stopping at the grocery on my way home. Is there anything I can get you?"

"Long as you've got coffee in the morning, I'll eat and drink anything. Thanks, honey."

"Good to have you here," she said. Lynn loved Polly's father, a calm, steady presence amidst chaos. And she suspected that there might be a bit of chaos for the next few weeks. She wondered how long he intended to stay.

CHAPTER 46

Between hosting Grangers, checking in on Polly and the baby, and keeping the Cottage running smoothly, Lynn's weeks were a blur. She had resolved to maintain some distance from Gus and she told him as much one morning, asking that he stop hovering and respect her need for space. She was, however, very loving to his children, letting Dulcie know that she was there if she needed her.

Jasper Larrabee's behavior had deteriorated since his baby sister came home from the hospital. He had been hitting the other children, even his buddy Ben. Thus, one of the three teachers was always "on Jasper duty," usually Rusty, whom the little boy adored. The first week of November was scheduled to be Polly's first week back. She was planning to do half days until Thanksgiving, and if all went well, she would return full-time after that. She often dropped Jasper off, the baby wrapped in a carrier on her chest. One morning in late October, the trio arrived, Jasper rushing in and tackling Ben as his friend sat playing trucks with Rusty.

"Jasper, no!" Polly said, rushing to his side, pulling him off Ben. "That's too rough!"

"Hate you, hate you," Jasper said, pulling away and running toward the kitchen.

Rusty started to rise, and Lynn put up her hand. "I'll go."

She caught Jasper at the kitchen door and gently took hold of his forearm.

"Lemme go!" he said, squirming and wriggling.

Lynn knelt in front of him, holding both arms now. "Jasper, that's enough."

He continued to whine and wriggle, refusing to meet her eyes, but Lynn held fast. Polly stood a short distance away, her arms cradling the baby carrier. Finally, he settled, collapsing to a heap on the floor. Lynn still held him, one hand grasping his arm, the other on one knee. "Jasper, we don't tackle our friends, do we? That's not safe." He ignored her, staring at the floor. "I can't let you go until I'm sure you're going to play safely. Do you understand?"

Nothing.

"Okay, then you'll be my special helper today, and we'll have to hold hands all day. Is that what you want?"

Jasper shook his head.

"Then what do you have to remember?"

"No tackling."

"What else?"

"No hitting."

"And be kind and safe with our friends, right?"

Jasper nodded.

"Do you want to go back and play with Ben and Rusty?"

Another nod.

"Okay, then." She released him, breathing a sigh of relief as Jasper walked to join the others and sat beside his friend, waiting to be asked to play.

"Thanks," Polly said, sitting on one of the sofas in the main room. "He's been really difficult, especially with me. Since Mom left, his naughty behavior has escalated. She took time to play with him, and he's missing that attention."

"Maybe you need some help?"

"His Aunt Ivy is coming for the first two weeks that I'm back."

"She's welcome to stay with me."

"Let's see how it goes. I was actually thinking I might leave the baby at home with her for the morning and bring Jasper myself. Then we'd trade off. When we get home, Jaspie gets Aunt Ivy all to himself. He's crazy about her."

"Can I help?"

"Thanks, but we're coping. How are you feeling?"

"Great. The nausea's finally gone, but my clothes are getting tight with this baby bump."

"You've never looked better," Polly said, smiling. "When do we start birthing classes, by the way?"

Lynn laughed. "You can't be serious with all you've got on your plate."

"I'm dead serious. Kev and I have already discussed it. They're at night, so he'll take care of the kids, and I'll be free."

"Are you sure, Poll? Barb has offered to come out. I was originally thinking after the baby, but I could have her come before."

"It's completely up to you," Polly said. "Even though you didn't get to be my coach, I'd love to be yours."

"Of course, the job is yours," Lynn said.

Polly beamed. "Can't wait. But I am always ready to step aside if a certain horse trainer wants to step in."

"No chance of that," Lynn said.

"What's up with you guys, anyway? I've been so consumed with the baby, Jasper, and my parents, we haven't had any time to catch up."

"Nothing's up. I told him the week after Julia was born that I needed space and I didn't want to confuse the kids. Gus continues to ask to see me, invites me to the house, whatever, but I've resisted. I try to be loving to the kids when they're here, but I don't want Dulcie hoping for something that's never going to happen."

"You don't know that."

"Yes, I do, Ms. Pollyanna."

"If you keep your distance, you're never going to find out, are you?"

"Honestly, it hurts too much to see him, and I'm not sure if this friends thing won't continue to hurt."

"Well, I'm still hoping," Polly said, patting her chest.

"Shush, here he comes," Lynn said as the door opened and Gus and kids stepped in.

As she always did, Dulcie ran to hug Lynn, then headed into the kitchen corner, where she liked to start her day. Cal toddled off to join Rusty and the boys.

"Morning, ladies," Gus said as he hung up backpacks and extracted lunches and water bottles. "Good to see you, Polly."

"Hi, Gus, good to see you too. I can't remember, have you met Julia?"

He smiled, peeking at the sleeping baby. "Kevin brought her out to the farm last week. She's a real cutie."

"That's right, I'd forgotten he did that. Well, guys, I've gotta run," Polly said, giving Lynn a sly look as she headed in to say goodbye to Jasper.

Never known for her subtlety, Lynn thought, watching her friend's retreat.

"How are you?" Gus asked, holding the kids' lunch bags.

"Here, I'll take those." Lynn grabbed them and headed for the kitchen.

He followed her. "Lynn, please, can we talk?"

"There's nothing to say. As I told you, I need time to figure out what this can and can't be." As she spoke, she waved her hand back and forth.

"Can't we try to figure it out together?"

"No."

"You look beautiful today. In fact, you look prettier every time I see you."

She raised both hands. "Don't do that, please."

"Lynn, I care about you and the baby."

She was about to respond when Daisy poked her head in. "Want us to start the project? Everything's out."

Lynn waved her hand. "I'll be right there." Daisy closed the door. "Gus, I can't do this right now."

She brushed by him and out of the room. As she plunged into the painting project, Gus kissed the kids and departed.

As she moved about the room, Daisy passed by and whispered, "I gotta tell you, that is the cutest dad we have."

"Hush, Daisy," Lynn said, unable to keep the irritation from her voice. *Cute indeed!*

CHAPTER 47

As Gus drove to work, he felt as if his heart had been ripped from his chest. The loss of Lynn weighed on him night and day. He wasn't sleeping, could barely eat, and was often distracted and irritable at work. Only with the horses or reading to the kids at night did he feel at ease. The rest of the time, he was miserable. *This can't go on,* he told himself. *You've got to make up your mind and do something, but what?*

As he drove up to the main barn, he spied the herd, already in the largest corral. They had rescued seventeen mustangs, half of them in deplorable condition. Their grazing land depleted, they had been starving, and now they had to be slowly reintroduced to food. He spent half of every day among the wild, frightened creatures and was slowly beginning to earn their trust. It would be at least a year before any of them would be ready for adoption. As he parked the truck, one of his favorites, Dusty, approached the fence, nickering softly.

"Hey, girl," he said, "Be right with you."

As he headed into the barn, his cell phone rang. As he pulled it out, he spied his father-in-law's name. "Jim?"

"Hi, son. Guess where I am?"

"Somewhere in Arizona heading our way, I hope."

"Just outside of Flagstaff. Have a couple of stops, but I should be to your area by late afternoon. Got room for an old man for the night?"

"Of course. The kids'll be thrilled. Do you need directions?"

"I should be fine. Just checked and your Valley Stables shows up on my GPS."

"Great. Well, if you make it down the drive, turn south or left and follow the drive past the stables, and our house is the only one in that direction."

They rang off, and Gus smiled. *At least Jim will be a distraction from my soap opera life.*

WHEN GUS AND THE KIDS DROVE UP TO THE HOUSE, HE SPIED JIM Olsen sitting in a porch rocker, legs stretched out on the railing. He waved and stood up, coming to greet them. "Howdy, partners," he said, opening his arms as Dulcie and Cal ran into them. "Quite a place you've got here."

"Let me put these inside," Gus said, holding the kids' backpacks. "Then we can give you the fifty-cent tour while it's still light."

They walked to the stables and introduced Jim to all the thoroughbreds, then their stablemates, the wild horses at the far end. "This is quite a project you've got goin' here," Jim said. "The Maynards have a small rescue program back home, but they never take more than one or two at a time."

"That's what they do at Morgan's Run. They train mustangs for use by the Border Patrol. I'll take you down there tomorrow."

"Impressive."

"Yeah, they've got three amazing trainers."

"None as good as you, I'll bet."

Gus grinned. "'Fraid you'd lose that bet. They've got a true horse whisperer down there. I'm gonna try and get him to come up and work with our guys once in a while. Guy's incredible."

"Papa, Papa, come see Dusty!" Dulcie called as the children reached the far stalls.

"Not too close, sweetie!" Gus called. "Remember, they're still wild."

Dulcie nodded as she stopped in front of Dusty's stall, barring Cal from drawing too close. Gus reached them and scooped up his son. The solid gray pony nickered softly, rubbing against the stall door. Before he could stop her, Dulcie reached up her hand and petted her nose. Gus shook his head. He might be earning the mustang's trust, but the connection between his daughter and Dusty was already love.

"You've got a budding horse whisperer right here," Jim said, patting Dulcie's head. The horse snorted and reared slightly as if wondering if Jim was a threat to the child.

"Okay, guys, better let Dusty go to sleep. Let's get Papa back to the house for some supper."

Later, after the children were asleep and the next day's lunches packed, Gus joined his father-in-law on the back porch. "What a view, even in the dark," Jim said. "And I thought we had stars in Jackson."

"It's pretty spectacular. Can I get you anything? Beer? Coffee? Seltzer?"

"Thanks, but I'm perfect."

Gus took a chair beside him. "It really is great to see you, Jim."

"The pleasure's mine. I miss you and the kids. So...how are you doin', son? You seem kind of glum. When Jeannie told me about your new lady, I figured I'd find you like a pig in shit, or at least happier than a year and a half ago."

"I've screwed up things with Lynn, and I'm dealing with the fallout."

"Not fixable?"

"Not without breaking my promise to Lissie, and I'm not sure I can do that."

"She was my sweet girl, but she always had a strong will. Knew what she wanted. She set her sights on you in kindergarten, didn't she?"

Gus smiled. "Yeah, I suppose she did. We both did. I miss that, you know? Having someone in your life who's known you that long, and loved you that long too."

"But it sounds like Lynn loves you and you her. Why would you turn your back on that? Can't expect everyone you meet and fall in love with to be a childhood friend."

"No, and she's a special woman for sure. Different from Lissie, but special in her own way."

"If those promises you made to my daughter are what's stopping you, Gus, you need to let go of 'em. I know my Lissie, and I know she'd want you to be happy."

"Did I tell you Lynn's pregnant?"

"All the more reason to marry her and be happy, son."

"But is that fair when I promised?"

"Listen here. Lissie was out of her mind those last few hours. After the baby was safely out, they drugged her up. When we said our goodbyes, she was already half gone. She didn't know what she was saying, poor baby."

"She sounded pretty clear to me," Gus said, even though he knew Jim was right. Lissie's eyes had been glazed and frightened.

"All I'm saying is that my Lissie, the Lissie I raised, would want you to be happy. If that meant marrying again, having more kids, anything you want, she'd be the first to say go for it. 'Don't look back, go forward.' That was one of her favorite expressions."

Gus smiled. "Carpe diem was another."

He grinned. "That's the spirit! Always knew her high school Latin would come in handy someday."

The two men talked for a while, then headed in, Jim to Gus's bed, Gus to the couch. When they said goodbye the next morning, Jim said, "Remember 'carpe diem' and be happy, Gus."

"I'll think about it. Thanks, Jim."

CHAPTER 48

"Hey, kids, hey, Mr. Casey," Daisy said, as they arrived at the Cottage.

"Morning," he said. They were the first arrivals and had walked in with Rusty. "Where's Lynn?"

"She has an appointment. She'll be in later. Not to worry. We have a small group today. Only your guys, Jasper, and Christy. The Morgans took the kids off for the day, and the babies are with their grandmothers on some sort of adventure," she said, referring to Charlotte Langdon and Lily Dillon.

"Okay, then," he said, hugging Dulcie and kissing the top of Cal's head. "Be good, kids. Have a great day."

"You too," Daisy called.

Gus hopped in the truck and pulled out his cell. Lynn answered on the first ring. "Hello?"

"Hey, I missed you at the Cottage. Are you okay?"

"Fine. I'm just coming in a little later today."

"Daisy said you had an appointment?"

Daisy has a big mouth, Lynn thought. "Just a routine doctor's appointment."

"With the obstetrician?"

"Yes."

He had a million things to do at work, but he heard himself saying, "Would you like me to come?"

"Are you asking because you'd like to come?"

"Yes."

She hesitated, then gave him the address. "It's at nine. I'm in town getting a muffin, then I'll head over."

"Meet you there."

THERE WAS AN AWKWARDNESS AS THEY SAT SIDE BY SIDE IN THE WAITING room, but when Dr. Gannon ran the Doppler over her belly and found the impossibly fast, tiny heartbeat, Lynn's eyes filled with tears and so did his. She reached over and took his hand.

"She's a beauty, folks," the diminutive doctor said. Lynn loved Dr. Gannon and had transferred to her practice after she delivered Julia. She reminded her of Linda Hunt, the actress, in her quirky, matter-of-fact manner and way of speaking.

"Yes, she is," Gus said, but he was looking at Lynn.

"Everything looks and sounds good," Dr. Gannon said. "Are you planning to go natural? Nancy can give you a list of upcoming classes. Ours are on Thursday evenings. You can jump in any time."

"Thanks, I'll grab a list on my way out," Lynn said, taking a tissue and wiping the jelly from her stomach before she pulled down her blouse. "Do you still think mid-March for a birth date?"

"From what you've told me and the baby's size, I'd say around the twentieth of March, give or take a week or two."

Gus waited while she checked out, and they walked to the parking lot together. "Thanks for letting me be here," he said, opening her car door for her.

"No thanks necessary," Lynn said, her emotions roiling. She knew if she didn't get in the car soon, she would burst into tears, and she couldn't, wouldn't do that in front of him. "I've gotta go."

"Wait, Lynn," he said, resting a hand on her door. "Could we have lunch, dinner, or a coffee sometime?"

"What's the point?" *Don't cry, don't cry!*

"I'd really like to talk to you and figure this out. I want to be in your life and the baby's."

"I'm not sure I can," Lynn said, her voice breaking.

"Can I call you?"

She nodded and backed away without another word. Several blocks down the street, her vision blurred with tears, and she pulled into Valley Hardware and stopped the car, sobbing. That was how Lang Dillon found her as he parked his Rover beside her SUV.

He tapped on the window. "Hey, Lynn, is that you?"

Oh great! Just what I need. "Hi, Lang. Yes, it's me."

His blue eyes were full of concern. "You okay?" In Lynn's eyes, Beth Morgan's tall, lanky husband was the handsomest man in the Valley. Except for Gus, of course.

"Yes, fine. I had a distressing phone call from my mom, that's all."

"I get you. Family can be stressful. Wanta grab a coffee or something?"

Lynn smiled at his kindness, realizing she must look like a wreck. "Thanks, but I've gotta get to work. I hear the grandmothers are taking the girls on an outing today."

"Yeah, they've gone to Tucson to the Reid Park Zoo."

"Lucky girls."

"You sure you're okay?"

"Positive, but thanks for checking."

"No problem. Have a good one."

Lynn dried her eyes as she watched him saunter into the hardware store. *What a great guy. Beth is very lucky.*

CHAPTER 49

Polly's first week back sailed by, and Lynn managed to avoid Gus. She might say a quick hello and goodbye, but she let Polly interact with him. On Friday, after saying hello to Dulcie and Cal, she disappeared into the kitchen and closed the door.

Gus watched her go, then turned sad eyes on Polly.

"Give her time," Polly said. "She's still grieving."

"That's why I want to see her. To find a way so she doesn't have to grieve and we can be together in some way."

"She wants the whole enchilada."

He nodded. "If she'd just see me."

"She'll get there. I'm sure she wants you in the baby's life. She just needs to figure out how. Right now, it hurts too much."

"That's it," he said, heading for the closed door. He pushed it open and found Lynn peeling carrots for their morning project. They were making stone soup after reading the children's book of the same name. She looked up when the door opened, then turned back to her work.

"You can't hide in here all morning."

"I'm not hiding."

"Look, Lynn, I know I'm an asshole and a whole lot of other things, but I have things I want to say to you."

She shook her head. "Not now, Gus, please."

"Okay, fine. Tomorrow, I've got Daisy babysitting. I have some work at the farm in the morning but will be coming into town at noon to pick up supplies. I would love you to join me for lunch at Gracie's. Twelve thirty, if you can get free?"

"I don't think so."

"Fine, but if you change your mind, I'll be in a back booth hoping to see you. If you don't come, I'll keep asking until you do. Have a good day." With that, he turned on his heel and walked out, before she could say a word.

A few minutes later, Polly poked her head in. "Hey, are you planning to stay in here all day?"

"Ha-ha."

"So?"

"So what?"

"So what did he want?"

"The same thing he always wants, to meet. For lunch at Gracie's tomorrow. Just what I need, another public display of blubbering for all the town to see."

"Maybe you won't blubber?"

"It seems to be all I do these days."

"I like that top, by the way. Where'd you get it?"

"Saguaro Dreams. They don't have a maternity section, but they have lots of these blousy tops, and they're cheap. I bought four. I'm also wearing my preggers jeans," she said, grinning as she lifted the hem of her pale green muslin blouse.

"Cool."

"Got 'em online. Two pairs and a skirt."

"I told you I have some things you can borrow!"

"And I said that nothing you have would fit unless I lose fifty pounds and change my body shape overnight."

"No way. Maternity clothes are very forgiving."

"Not this forgiving," Lynn said. "On a good day, I wear a twelve or fourte. What are you, a two? Come on, let's get the kids together. Do you want to read *Stone Soup* while I keep prepping?"

"No, you read, Daisy can take over here, and Rusty'll help with cleanup and then corral everyone. I've gotta pump, and I'll be back out in time for soup mixing."

"Sounds good."

"And Lynn, want my advice?"

"If it concerns you know who, not especially."

"Well, I'm giving it anyway. See him. Listen. Make a plan so that he doesn't keep upsetting you and all this," Polly said, waving her arms around, "gets resolved. You can't keep running into the kitchen every day at drop-off and dismissal."

"Ha-ha," Lynn said, smiling as Polly grabbed her bag of supplies for pumping her breast milk.

CHAPTER 50

The morning had been hectic, and he hated to leave the kids, but they loved Daisy. At least it was a beautiful day so they'd be out on their new swing set, picnicking in the backyard, and having a ball. As he drove past the house on his way to town, he caught sight of them chasing each other in the yard, Daisy in hot pursuit. *Another thing to work out,* he thought, watching the redhead. On more than one occasion, including this morning, Daisy had made it very clear to him that she was interested in seeing him. Daisy could not be described as subtle. *I'll have a talk with her this afternoon,* he resolved, heading up the drive toward the main road.

Lynn had spent a restless night trying to decide what to do about lunch with Gus. Finally, she resolved to go and was sitting in a back booth when he walked in. The look of surprise on his face made her smile. There was something ingenuous and endearing about Gus Casey, even if he had broken her heart.

"You came. I assumed you wouldn't, so I was just gearing up to eat alone."

Lynn smiled. "I can always leave. There's still time."

He put up his hands, "No, please." He slid into the booth, a grin on his face. "It's so good to see you."

"It's only been a day," she replied, thinking to herself, *Keep up the light banter, and I might make it through without breaking down.*

"You know what I mean," he said, eyes serious. "You look really pretty today. I mean, you always look pretty, but especially now."

"Thanks." *You look gorgeous too. You always do.*

"Hey, folks, good to see you." Gracie the owner interrupted them, pad in hand, apron stained with a mysterious pink liquid. "You know what you want?"

"I'll take a Gila burger and fries," Lynn said. "And an iced tea."

"Sounds good to me," Gus said. "Make it two."

"You got it. Maria'll be over directly with your teas."

When Gracie disappeared, Lynn said, "I'm going to try really hard not to get emotional. I've been doing that a lot lately."

Gus smiled. "So, I have an idea. Why don't we talk about day-to-day stuff now, then we can go across to the park after? Does that sound okay?"

She nodded. "You've got this all planned out, don't you?"

"Sort of," he said, smiling. "So tell me what's new. How are you doing? The Cottage? Whatever?"

"Well, one thing I know is that Daisy has a huge crush on you."

He laughed. "I'm going to nip that in the bud when I get home today."

The mention of Daisy and her crush lightened the mood, and they spent an enjoyable meal catching up. Lynn had missed him and the easy way they had of finishing each other's sentences and understanding without words the issues the other described. Her body ached for his arms around her, and she thought back to the hospital when he held her so tenderly. *And now, here he is. The man I'm crazy in love with, and I can't touch him, kiss him. Sheer torture!*

Finally, Gus paid the check, and they strolled across to the park. There were a few families playing on the grass and swings, so he suggested they head for a bench at the far end near the wooded area that led to hiking trails. "This okay?" he asked, gesturing to the bench.

Lynn sat, and he sat beside her. He cleared his throat. "I've been all over the place, literally and figuratively, since June, and I'd like to share some of it with you, but not now. This moment is for me to say something I'd rather have said over a romantic dinner at the Red Mesa or some secluded locale."

Lynn gazed at him, wary but curious. "You made it pretty clear in August that that kind of relationship is impossible for us."

"That's what I want to say. I was wrong. Completely wrong. What we had is precious and rare. I let it slip through my fingers because of a promise I made in the past. A promise to someone I loved very much, but who is no longer here. I gave that promise so that Lissie would be calm when she went into surgery. I didn't want her last moments before anesthesia to be agitated. However, with help from a few wise people and a lot of soul-searching, I've made peace with the recognition that the Lissie I knew would never expect nor want me to keep that promise. Maybe for a few years to mourn her passing, but Lissie would want me and the kids to move on. I know she would.

"It's difficult when there's only been one significant other in one's life. It's hard to imagine how you can live without that person. I was still wondering this year until I met you. Lynn, there are many things I don't know, but what I do know is I love you, and I cannot imagine living without you."

Gus slipped from the bench onto one knee. He pulled a small blue velvet box from his jacket pocket. "I don't expect an answer now, and I know it'll take a long time before you can find it in your heart to forgive me, if you can? But I wanted to ask now, so you can think about it. Lynn Manguilli, will you marry me?"

Lynn had been listening quietly, not sure what to expect until he slid down to his knee. Now she was too shocked to speak. "Gus... I...I can't... I don't know what to say."

He hopped up, sitting back down beside her. Taking her hand, he opened it and placed the velvet box on her palm, folding her fingers around it. "I figured you'd be surprised. Please don't feel you have to say anything now. If you consent to keep this and think about my proposal, that's enough for me."

Lynn felt numb and wasn't sure whether she should laugh or cry. "But what about your promise?"

"I can explain later, but for now, let's focus on us. I can see by those tears in your beautiful dark eyes that I've upset you, the last thing I want to do."

"Not upset, just surprised. I've spent the past two months trying very hard to let go of what we had and to reach some kind of peace. I'm not sure I can go back." As she spoke, she fingered the tiny box, and the clasp sprang open to reveal a dark emerald surrounded by tiny diamonds in an antique setting. "Oh, it's so beautiful. My birthstone."

"I know, I asked Polly."

"She knows about this?"

"No, I just asked if your birthday was coming up and she told me it was the fourth of May."

Softly she closed the box. "I can't promise anything, but I will think about what you've asked. I want you to hang on to this until I decide." She handed him the box.

Gus forced a smile. "Okay, then."

Lynn watched as he tucked the box in his pocket. She knew him well enough to know that he was deeply disappointed yet trying not to show it. "I'm sorry, Gus."

"Nothing for you to be sorry about. Can I walk you to your car? Would you like an ice cream? Lemonade?"

"No, thanks. I'm kind of tired. I've been taking naps on the weekends. Don't seem to have as much energy." Lynn stood.

"Glad to hear that you're taking care of yourself."

"Oh, Gus," she said, opening her arms.

Neither wanted to let go, and Lynn knew that she needed to make the first move. "I should go," she said softly.

"Of course." He stepped back and took her hand.

CHAPTER 51

Lynn opened her front door and stepped into the quiet of her condo. Still numb, she sat at the kitchen counter staring into space. *He loves you. He's asked you to marry him.* She wondered if she had dreamed the whole thing. And then she was crying, tears of joy and release. Not in a million years had she expected this today. She had spent weeks gearing up for a conversation full of negotiation and planning about custody and parental rights. She knew Gus. He'd made a promise, and he was going to keep it. It was actually one of the qualities she loved best about him.

She poured herself a glass of water and took her phone to the sofa. It was her intention to phone Polly, but then she stopped herself. Instead she scrolled down to her mother's number.

"Hi, sweetheart, what a lovely surprise."

Mother and daughter had not spoken in several weeks, and during their last conversation, Lynn had been a sobbing mess after Polly's near death and the ongoing pain of dealing with Gus. During that call, Sorcha had recommended she take a breather and maybe find a therapist. Lynn had a name from Maggie Morgan, but had not yet made an appointment.

Without preamble, she launched into a description of Gus's

proposal and her state the past several weeks. When she was finished, she said, "Oh, Momma, please tell me what to do."

"Honey, I wish I could, but this is *your* decision. Do you love him?"

"Beyond all reason, or at least I did. I don't know... I'm scared. I can't go back to that dark hole if he changes his mind."

"Is that likely?"

"No."

"Then you need to decide what you want. Is it life with this man, or have you already moved on?"

"Moved on? I could never love anyone like I love Gus."

"There you have it, then. Your answer."

"Is it?" Lynn asked, feeling calmer and more peaceful.

"Only you can answer that, darling."

"Thanks, Mom. How's everything back there?"

"Same ole, same ole. Your sister's got a new boyfriend. Rolf. We're not crazy about him, but she seems to be. Time will tell."

They talked awhile longer, then Lynn rang off. She went into the bedroom, closed her eyes, and slept.

After a restless night of tossing and turning, she rose Sunday morning achy and out of sorts. She dressed in jeans, a sweatshirt, and hiking shoes. The condo was a short distance from several trailheads, and she decided to take the easy river trail that led south, eventually passing Morgan's Run and the Dillons' vineyards. It was a bright morning, the air crisp and cool, skies clear blue as far as the eye could see. "Just what I need," she said aloud as she grabbed her small day pack from the backseat. Smiling, she patted her belly. "Correction, just what we need."

Her plan was to walk until the trail met the Morgan's Loop Trail, then turn back, a distance of six miles or so. As she walked, small parties of hikers, joggers, and mountain bikers passed by on the popular trail. She was almost to the Loop when she spied two joggers approaching. As they drew near, keeping a moderate loping pace, she recognized Lang and Beth and waved.

"Hey, guys. Beautiful day. I didn't know you were a jogger, Beth."

Beth grinned. "Very part-time, not like this guy." She patted her husband's shoulder. "Taking advantage of the day and generous grandparents. Lang's parents have our sweetheart this morning." She touched her belly as Lang handed her a water bottle. "Gotta keep in shape for the baby and running after Lily."

Lynn nodded. "I hear ya."

Lang looked from one to the other. "If I'm not mistaken, you ladies are due at about the same time, right?"

"I'm mid-March," Lynn said.

Beth smiled. "March second, according to my doctor. She loves to predict down to the minute."

"Mine too. Who do you see?"

"Gannon, but I'm hoping to deliver with her midwife, Pippa."

"Yeah? I've seen Pippa once and liked her."

"Pippa's terrific," he said. "How you doing anyway?"

Lynn gazed over at Lang before turning to Beth. "Your poor husband had the misfortune to run into me the other day when I was a blubbering mess. Hormones, life, whatever had caught up to me."

Beth gave her a warm smile. "Believe me, he's seen much worse."

Lang grinned. "Anytime, ladies. Bring it on."

They chatted for a few more minutes, then said their goodbyes. Lynn walked a short distance and turned in time to see the couple disappear around a bend in the trail. *That's what I want. Someone to care for me, hand me my water bottle, love me. And I know who that someone is. Without question.*

She walked a half mile farther, then turned back toward home. She did not meet Lang and Beth again, so she assumed they had taken the bike path that ran through town, then south along the Gila Highway. When she got home, she showered, then sat on the deck with a lemonade. About a half hour later, she thought, *What are you waiting for, Lynn Manguilli?*

She hopped up, put her empty glass in the sink, and headed out again.

CHAPTER 52

G us and the kids were in the backyard. The kids were on the jungle gym, and he sat in the shade reading the newspaper. He was interrupted from time to time for a push on the swings, but he mostly sat and watched his beautiful children. His and Lissie's children. So happy in their new home. His heart ached for Lynn. Her rejection of his proposal stung, even though he understood. *Get over it, buddy. You were an asshole. Quit moping around. These guys need all of you.*

It was at that moment that Dulcie cried out, "Lynn!" His daughter jumped from the swing and hit the ground running. Incredulous, he turned and spied Lynn coming around the side of the house.

Her cheeks were rosy, and she was in jeans and a Morgan's Run sweatshirt, the bump of her belly apparent as she moved. As he rose to greet her, Gus thought she had never looked lovelier. "Hey, this is a surprise. Did you tell me you were coming and I forgot?"

"No, it's kind of a spur-of-the-moment thing. Sorry, that's not true. I've been mulling it over for eighteen hours." She bent down and scooped Dulcie up for a hug.

"Oh?"

Lynn smiled at the man who had captured her heart so completely, the gorgeous, loving father who was staring at her with what appeared to be confusion and maybe hope in his soft green eyes. She held his wisp of a daughter in her arms, the little girl she already loved as her own. Oblivious to the three of them, Cal toddled toward the sandbox, waving a plastic truck.

There is nowhere on earth I'd rather be, she thought as Gus approached.

"Can Lynn stay for lunch, Daddy? Please, can she stay?"

"She can stay forever as far as I'm concerned."

"I was hoping you'd say that."

"You were?"

Confused, Dulcie gazed from Lynn to her father. "Is Lynn moving in with us?"

"Hey, Dulce, why don't you go play with your brother and let Lynn and me talk?"

"No, it's okay," Lynn said, holding the child in her arms. "Dulcie, your daddy asked me a really important question yesterday and I wanted to come out today to give him my answer. Is that okay?"

The little girl scrunched up her nose. "What question? What question?"

"Dulcie, let Lynn talk."

"Yes."

"Yes, you want to talk?"

"No, my answer is yes."

"Yippee!" he cried, swooping them both into his arms. "You've made me the happiest man alive, Lynn Manguilli!"

"What question? What question?" Dulcie asked, giggling as her father spun them around.

"Okay, wait right here," he said, setting them down. "I'll be right back."

They watched him race into the house and reappear within seconds, holding something in his left hand.

"What, Daddy, what?"

Gus grinned as he led Lynn to the chair in the shade. "Here, I'll show you. Dulce, you stand right there." He placed her beside the chair, then went down on one knee. "Lynn, I love you, my darling girl. Will you marry me?"

"I love you too," she said, fingers tracing his jawline as she turned to Dulcie, who stood openmouthed, staring. "And I love you, Dulcie Casey, and Cal too. I love you all and want to marry you more than anything else in the world."

Gus pulled her into his arms, kissing her as Dulcie jumped on their shoulders, screaming, "Yay! Yay! I got my wish!"

Laughing, Gus grabbed his daughter, tickling her in the grass before turning to Lynn. "Are you sure about this?"

"Never surer of anything in my life."

"That's my girl," he said, kissing her softly. "That's my girl. And, oh golly, have I missed this."

"Me too."

EPILOGUE

"This has been a wonderful honeymoon," Lynn said, her head resting on his shoulder. They were about to head home after two nights at the Vermillion guesthouse. About a quarter mile from the main farm and restaurant, the tiny cottage was a quiet retreat with its crisp white linens, simple pine furnishings, and luxurious bath. Lynn had sighed with pleasure when they stepped into the beautiful space two days ago, a spacious claw-foot tub just visible through the bathroom door.

"Finally, we get to take a bath together!" she'd said, and here they were, two days later, after several baths, soaking one last time before they dressed to go home.

Gus took her hand, kissing each of her fingers. "Too short."

"Just right."

"Maybe next year when the baby's weaned, we can go for a week somewhere?"

"I'd like that," she said, smiling as she felt his arousal against her back. "I also like what I'm feeling at this very minute." She turned halfway round and kissed him.

"Want to fool around?" he asked, cupping her breasts.

"Oh, is that what we're doing? Fooling around?"

"I hope so. Now come closer and let me make love to you, Ms. Casey."

Lynn turned and straddled him, opening herself to guide him in. She leaned back and arched her spine, reveling in the pleasure of fullness with him deep inside her. They began to move in perfect synchrony, their mounting hunger for one another blocking all reason, obliterating all thought. As they climaxed, water swirling all around them, she screamed in ecstasy as Gus murmured, "I know, baby, I know."

A few minutes later as he cradled her in his arms, his hand resting on her belly, Lynn said, "Do you think Edna would mind if we take this tub with us?"

"No need, my beautiful wife. I called Kevin yesterday, and he's gonna start scouting around for one."

"What?" She sat up.

"Yup, apparently they're hard to find, but he uses a lot of salvage places, and he's pretty sure he can locate one."

"Where are you going to put it?"

"In the bathroom extension. I already cleared it with the bosses. We're gonna extend the master bedroom to give you a space of your own, a small study or whatever you want. And, while we're at it, I thought why not add enough space for a closet and tub."

"But it's not even yours."

"Ours, you mean?"

"Yes, I like the sound of that."

"Well, it will be ours soon. Spark and Ben agreed to sell me the house and ten acres. It's home for the kids now. My home and yours."

Lynn wrapped her arms around his neck. "Oh, Gus Casey, I love you!"

He captured her lips in a soft, wet kiss. "This water's getting kind of chilly, but what if we continue this in that nice warm bed?"

She reached down, stroking him, and said, "Why, Mr. Casey, that's an even better idea than a claw-foot tub!"

~

Updates about future releases, please visit my AUTHOR WEBSITE and sign up for my Newsletter and Follow me on BookBub!

Please read on for lots of Morgan celebrations in the sample chapters of *A Valley Christmas!*

A VALLEY CHRISTMAS

Chapter 1

The cry of a hawk startled Leonora Morgan awake. As she wondered what prey had eluded the raptor, she stirred and turned to the clock. Then, with a sigh, she leaned back on the pillows to gaze at her husband still fast asleep. *As handsome as the day we met*, she thought, reaching over to smooth back his thick salt-and-pepper hair.

Their fortieth anniversary, the wedding of their son, Kyle, *and* Christmas were less than a week away, and she had a million things to do. She snuggled deeper into the mass of down pillows and let her mind drift back to a crisp fall day in California.

~

As she walked across campus with her dearest friend, Suzie Miller, they met Spark and Patsy Foster. Newlywed twenty-one-year-olds, Spark and Patsy had married a week earlier against the wishes of both of their families. Patsy came from money, Spark did not, but he was well on his way to making his fortune in alternative energy. An engineering major, the previous summer he had experimented with methanol, which had bombed. Now he was investing heavily in solar.

"Hey, ladies, glad we met you," Patsy said, smiling at Suzie, whom she knew well. Leonora had only met the perky redhead once. "We're having a small wedding celebration tomorrow night, and we'd love for you both to join us."

Alongside the newlyweds stood a tall, lanky young man with eyes the color of cornflowers and chestnut hair thick and tousled as if he'd just hopped out of bed. His eyes never left Leonora, a gentle, steady gaze that felt warm and comfortable. *Like the home I've had never had,* she mused.

"That sounds fun," Suzie said, smiling at her friend. "You remember Nora?"

"Sure we do," Patsy said, eyes twinkling as she gazed at Leonora. "And this is Spark's best friend, Ben Morgan."

"I've seen you," Suzie gushed, stepping forward to shake his hand. "Will you be at the party?"

"You bet," he replied, smiling at Suzie, then turning to Leonora. "Pleased to meet you, Nora."

As Ben Morgan shook her hand, Leonora's knees wobbled and she felt light-headed. His hand trembled as it grasped hers. When she looked up, she was startled to glimpse a depth of feeling in his eyes.

"Yes, hi, you too," she finally managed to sputter. *Drop-dead gorgeous, that's what he is.* Completely unlike any of the men she knew. Lanky and solid, Ben wore jeans, a collared dress shirt open at the neck, and scuffed cowboy boots. Different pair, but the same brand he still wore today. He towered over her at six feet six, as did his handsome best friend, Spark. Even as a young man, Spark was often mistaken for the actor Fred Thompson.

Ben shook her hand. Later, he told her that his first sight of her had hit him like a lightning bolt and he knew right then that he was looking at the woman with whom he would spend his life. About a foot shorter than him, she was slender, with full, rounded breasts. She wore a short pencil skirt and matching green cashmere sweater. *And oh those legs!*

"Please say you'll both come," Patsy said, squeezing her husband's arm. "It would mean so much to us."

"Of course we'll come, won't we, Nora?" Suzie said, looking from Patsy to her.

"Of course." Leonora nodded, afraid to look up into those blue eyes again.

~

Drawing her back from her remembering, Ben reached for her. "Hey, beautiful, good morning."

"Hey, yourself."

"Penny for your thoughts."

"Well, if you must know, I was thinking back to Stanford and the first time I set eyes on a certain handsome cowboy."

He chuckled. "Country bumpkin next to Ms. Bel Air Sophisticate."

"Yet you still managed to sweep me off my feet and carry me off to the valley you couldn't stop talkin' about."

"Desperate times require desperate measures. 'Sides, I was afraid if I stopped talking, you'd get bored and walk away. The Valley was the only topic I could say more than two syllables about."

"Well, we know that's not true. Desperate?"

"Couldn't imagine livin' another day without you."

"And, now here we are. Forty years later."

"Blink of an eye, darlin'. Wouldn't change a second."

"Nor would I," she said, smiling as she slid down beside him.

"That's more like it." He kissed her as he drew her into his arms.

"Mmm," she said. "Someone's perky this morning."

"Always."

After four decades, the elder Morgans were more in love with each other than ever, still learning what gave the other pleasure. This morning was no different as his gentle, rough hands moved under her satin night shirt to caress Leonora's magnificent, full breasts. As he trailed kisses from her lips, down her long slender neck, she unbuttoned her top and moved against him.

As her husband took one breast, then the other into his mouth, tongue circling, teasing her nipples, she murmured, "Oh, sweetie, you're still pushing all my buttons. Please, please, put me out of my misery." As she spoke, Leonora's hands caressed him, then slid his boxers down over his hips, casting them aside with her toes.

"Gladly," he said, gently parting her legs and entering her. *Home,* he sighed as they moved as one toward a tremulous, loving climax.

After, as they lay entwined, he kissed the tip of her nose and said the same words he uttered every time they made love. "Thanks, darlin'."

"You're welcome, cowboy," she said, responding as she always did.

"You ready for the big parties?"

"I'd rather stay here and snuggle with you," she said, settling into the crook of his shoulder.

"That's what I like to hear."

"But, there are lists a mile long, Ben. Are you sure we should be doing this along with Kyle and Harriet's wedding? I hate to steal their thunder."

"No danger of us ole fogies stealing thunder or anything else from those two young firecrackers, darlin'."

"I suppose not, but there's so much to do. Yikes, that list is long! Then there's the celebration for Gail and Tim and the rehearsal dinner! Not to mention Christmas! Thank goodness we decorated early. That's done, at least. I want everything to be super special."

"It will be. Vermillion'll do a great job with the party for Gail and Tim," he said, referring to a nearby farm-to-table restaurant. "And Friday night's a barbecue. Spark has Aria and her crew handling all that," he added, referring to their dear friend and his chef Aria Firorelli.

"I know, I know... That's what we should have said about our party: low key!"

He grinned, hand massaging her back. "How many people are comin' to this shindig?"

"About a hundred."

"Hmm...a little more than low key by Valley standards, but not too much for our crew."

"Ever the optimist." She kissed his cheek. "That's why I love you so much."

Instead of rising immediately, Leonora lay back down and snuggled against him.

"What's wrong, sweetheart?"

"I was just thinking back to what a snob I was."

"Never."

"Yes, I was. Awful."

"Don't remember any such thing."

"Yes, you do, because you were the one reining me in. Think how nasty I was about Maggie when Ben started dating her."

"You love your children, that's all."

"Oh, pish tush." She gave him a peck on the cheek as she moved away and sat up. "You have a blind spot where I'm concerned. Always have."

"Always will."

She smiled. "I love you, Ben Morgan."

"Right back at you, darlin'."

As she stood, Leonora grabbed the side table, faltering.

"That's it. We're gonna see the doc."

"It's just my pesky old knee."

"It's more than that, honey, and you know it. You used to love to ride, but you haven't gone near Misty for three years."

"Misty is busy enough with all the lessons and pony camps," she said, referring to her beautiful white Andalusian, an anniversary gift from her husband years ago.

"That's not the point, and you know it. You hurt, and I hurt for you."

"Let's talk about this later. Okay? I've got a million and one things to do." She leaned over, kissed his forehead, then disappeared into the bathroom, forestalling any further discussion.

Chapter 2

"You sure you're okay with this, babe?" Kyle asked as they settled in the plane for the trip west.

Harriet smiled. "What? Getting married?"

"Ha-ha. No, I meant with the wedding at the ranch and the whole triple event with my parents' anniversary and the celebration for Gail and Tim."

She leaned over and kissed him. "Of course I'm okay with it. Mom's keyed, and my sisters can't wait to see the Valley."

"I just don't want anything to steal your special day."

Her hand grazed his cheek, tracing a line along his firm, handsome jaw. "My special day happened the day we met. Now, if you're standing beside me, that's all that matters. You know I'm not much of a limelight person."

"You okay about your dad being there?"

Her face clouded, and Harriet frowned. "He wanted to come. I didn't feel I could say no."

"But I can. To protect you and your mom."

Harriet smiled at him, hand gently caressing his jawline. "It's okay, my champion. Mom's strong, and I've made my peace with it and Dad. As you know, my wicked stepmother is coming too, since she's *dying to see the Valley.'* She'll have to babysit him."

Kyle gazed at his fiancée, who rarely spoke harshly about anyone. He had only met her dad once, and the impression he took away was of a depressed, late-middle-aged dreamer. Rita had been traveling at the time, so he had not yet met Jud Morgan's second wife. "Where are they staying?"

"The Lodge," she said, referring to the large inn and spa on his parents' ranch, Morgan's Run. "They don't get in until Friday afternoon, thank goodness. And they'll be gone early Sunday."

"They the only ones at the Lodge?"

"No, Frankie's there. She can handle Dad and Rita. Most of Tim's family are at the Lodge. The only other Yarners coming are Tim's aunt Grace and Mavis, and they're there. My guess is Dad and Rita will be so intimidated by that crowd that they'll keep a low profile." The Darn Yarners, including Frankie Brown and Harriet's mom,

Helen, were a group of dear friends from the village of Horseshoe Crab Cove, friends who had supported and loved each other for many years.

"Karen's with you at Spark's, right?"

"Yup. Remarkably, Spark's managed to fit Karen and most of my family since he has a million bedrooms. What about your friends? I have to admit I haven't been keeping up with the guest list."

Kyle smiled, reaching over to take her hand and squeezing it. "Why would you with my mother in charge? I only have a couple comin' from vet school and my college roommate, John. John's staying with Beth and Lang, and the two vet school buddies are at the Lodge too."

"It's gonna be fine, isn't it?" she asked as the plane took off.

"Course it is, babe." *If your father behaves.*

"So what can Maggie and I do?" Ben Morgan asked. "Kids are at the Cottage right now and Mag's at the stables, but we can do airport runs, get food in. Anything you need."

His parents sat at the dining room table enjoying a late lunch. "Thanks, honey," Leonora said. "I think we're set for now. Spark has ordered a fleet of cars for the week, and they'll be running to and from the airport. Between Aria and her crew and Carmela, the food is well in hand. Johnny arrives tomorrow, and he'll be a huge help." She referred to chef Johnny Stockdale, who ran the kitchen for Emma's Dream, the ranch's summer camp for handicapped children.

"Remind me who's staying with us," her son asked.

"Richard's daughter Ava and her family. Their children will have such fun with Emma and Bennie."

"We're excited. Who's here with you guys?" Her dark-haired, handsome son looked from one to the other.

"Just Kyle and Harriet, her sister Hazel, and Sam and Rose. We're holding out the last two bedrooms for stragglers," Ben Senior said. "We wish we could have everyone here."

"I can't wait to meet my next precious grandbaby," Leonora said.

"Maggie was surprised she's traveling now," her son said.

"Doctors have their own rules, I guess," Ben Senior replied. "Maybe she'll have a Valley baby."

"We'd sure love it." Leonora grasped the table as she rose on shaky legs.

"You okay, Mom?"

"Fine, fine. Just a little stiff."

Ben Senior observed her but said nothing.

His son stood. "Well, okay, then, I've gotta get movin'. I've got some errands in town, then I'll pick up the kids and head back to greet everyone."

"Dinner's at the Lodge tonight," his father said. "See you all later." When the door closed behind their son, he turned to his wife, who was stacking their lunch plates. "Okay, let's talk, darlin'."

"Didn't I tell you later?"

"This is later, and I can't sit by and watch you limping around. You wince every time you stand up."

Leonora waved her hand. "It's nothing. Just a funny range-of-motion issue. When all the festivities are over, I'll get it checked out."

Ben frowned. "I'd rather you do it now."

"Didn't slow me down this morning, did it?" She winked at him as she headed for the kitchen.

Ben followed her as she handed the lunch things to Carmela, their cook and housekeeper. "Can we talk about this Nora? I'm serious."

"Thanks, Carm," she said, leading the way to the back terrace, where she sat on a bench in the shade. She patted the seat beside her, and he sat down. "There's nothing to say. It's this," she said, raising her legs out straight in front of her. "I can't get them farther apart than this. That's why I can't get on a horse, and I wouldn't feel comfortable riding even if I managed to somehow hoist myself into the saddle."

"You haven't wanted to ride for at least a year."

"You were more accurate this morning. Three years."

"So this has been comin' on?"

She nodded.

"Why didn't you tell me?"

"I kept thinking it would get better. You know I do my stretching every morning and yoga."

"I'm gonna call Lang and get a recommendation for an orthopedic doc. Today. They interact with those fellas all the time through Rambler Sports."

"That's not necessary. Besides, I don't want the kids to know," she said, tears rimming her eyes.

"I'll ask Lang to keep it quiet."

"He'd better. Besides, I'm just getting old, that's all."

He reached over to envelop her in his strong arms. "Never, darlin'. You look as young as you did the day we met and even more beautiful."

Leonora smiled. "Then we'd better make an appointment for you to see an eye doctor."

"So do I have the go-ahead to call Lang?"

She nodded. "Okay, but hush, hush, hush. And no interfering with any of the party planning and events. Promise?"

"Promise," he said, kissing the tip of her nose. "I love you, Nora."

"Right back at you," she said, hugging him.

Get *A Valley Christmas!*

ALSO BY M. LEE PRESCOTT

Contemporary Romance

Mystery

The Ricky Steele Mysteries

Prepped to Kill

Gadfly

Lost in Spindle City

Poof!

Lady Love: A Cautionary Tale

Also, featuring Ricky Steele:

Jigsaw

Roger and Bess Mysteries

A Friend of Silence

In the Name of Silence

The Silence of Memory

Silencing the Pen

Well-Loved Romances

Widow's Island

Hestor's Way

Morgan's Run Romances

Emma's Dream

Lang's Return

Jeb's Promise

Rose's Choice

Hope's Wonder

Ruthie's Love

Polly's Heart

Kyle's Journey

Gus' Home

A Valley Christmas

Aria's Song

Tom's Ride

Bella's Touch

Morgan's Fire Romances

Lucy's Hearth

Tim's Hands

Pam's Garden

Rich's Dilemma

Lolly's Wish

Greta's Goat

A Horseshoe Crab Cove Christmas

Joe's Calling

Young Adult Historical Romance

Song of the Spirit

A NOTE FROM THE AUTHOR

I am so happy to bring you Gus and Lynn's love story! This marks the ninth of the **Morgan's Run** books and also previews number ten, *A Valley Christmas*. If you run out of Morgan's run books, the spin-off series, **Morgan's Fire** follows Helen, Harriet, and a host of strong, resilient women across the country to the New England coastal town of Horseshoe Crab Cove! Stay tuned for updates about both series and the mysteries as well! Thank you so much for reading *Gus's Home* and returning with me to Saguaro Valley. As you know, the **Morgan's Run** books are set in the gorgeous American Southwest, an area of the country that is dear to my heart not only because it was home to my youngest son and family, but also because its beauty is so extraordinary and so startlingly different from that of my New England home. I am also excited to explore the beauty of the craggy New England coast with a village of colorful, vibrant characters Horseshoe Crab Cove (**Morgan's Fire).**

If you like *Gus's Home* and would be willing to write an Amazon review, I would be very grateful. If you would like to sign up for future book releases, giveaways, and occasional notices about my books, please visit my Author Website *http://www.mleeprescott.com/* and sign up for my newsletter and follow me on BookBub *https://www.book-bub.com/search/authors?search=M.+Lee+Prescott*. I promise I will not share your address, nor will I flood you with emails. Do visit my site to read more about my books and hear what's next.

Finally, this book has been revised, proofed, and edited many, many times, but my intrepid assistants and I are human, so if you spot a typo, please email me at *mleeprescott@gmail.com,* and I will fix it. If you'd like to know more about my other books, please scroll ahead to the next section.

Warm wishes,

M. Lee

ABOUT THE AUTHOR

M. Lee Prescott is the author of
dozens of works of fiction for adults,
young adults, and children, among
them *Prepped to Kill*, *Gadfly*, *Lost in
Spindle City*, and *Poof!* (Ricky Steele
Mysteries), *A Friend of Silence*, *In the
Name of Silence*, and *The Silence of
Memory* (Roger and Bess Mysteries),
Jigsaw, and *Song of the Spirit*, and her
newest contemporary romance
series, Morgan's Run, of which *Gus's
Home* is the ninth! She is thrilled to

be launching book eight in her Morgan's Fire series December 2022!
Three of her nonfiction titles have been published by Heinemann,
and she has published numerous articles in the field of literacy
education. Lee is a professor emeritus at a small New England liberal
arts college, where she taught reading and writing pedagogy. Her
current research focuses on mindfulness and connections to reading
and writing. She regularly teaches abroad, most recently in
Singapore.

Lee has lived in southern California (loved those Laguna nights!),
Chapel Hill, North Carolina, and various spots in Massachusetts and
Rhode Island. Currently, she resides in Massachusetts on a beautiful
river, where she canoes, swims, and watches an incredible variety of
wildlife pass by. She is the mother of two grown sons and spends lots
of time with them, their beautiful wives, and her beloved

grandchildren. When not teaching or writing, Lee's passions revolve around family, yoga (Kripalu is a second home), swimming, sharing mindfulness with children and adults, and walking.

Lee loves to hear from readers. Email her at *mleeprescott@gmail.com*, and visit her website to hear the latest and sign up for her newsletters!

Visit my author website and sign up for my newsletter at
http://www.mleeprescott.com

Follow me on BookBub *https://www.bookbub.com/search/authors? search=M.+Lee+Prescott*

If you have five minutes, please review this book!